"Boy, I could have used a guy like you back in Philly," Lainey said.

Something inside Tucker shifted, making his heart suddenly feel warmer, heavier, fuller. He realized he'd like nothing better than to come to her rescue. "Anytime, anywhere."

"Beware of offers made in haste," she warned, but her wry tone was undercut with a huskiness that sizzled a path straight to his heart.

"I won't ever regret this one," he said softly.

She started to turn away, but something in her eyes, some flicker of vulnerability that pained him even more for being the cause of it, had him reaching out and touching her chin. "I didn't mean to make you uncomfortable," he said. "And it wasn't a line. I know we just met, but I meant what I said, Lainey."

His gaze dropped to her lips and it was all he could do not to lower his mouth and let his kiss explain what he could not. He dragged his gaze back to hers. "If there is anything I can ever do, all you have to do is ask."

WHAT ARE *LOVESWEPT* ROMANCES?

They are stories of true romance and touching emotion. We believe those two very important ingredients are constants in our highly sensual and very believable stories in the LOVE-SWEPT line. Our goal is to give you, the reader, stories of consistently high quality that may sometimes make you laugh, sometimes make you cry, but are always fresh and creative and contain many delightful surprises within their pages.

Most romance fans read an enormous number of books. Those they truly love, they keep. Others may be traded with friends and soon forgotten. We hope that each LOVESWEPT romance will be a treasure—a "keeper." We will always try to publish

LOVE STORIES YOU'LL NEVER FORGET
BY AUTHORS YOU'LL ALWAYS REMEMBER

The Editors

TEASE ME

DONNA
KAUFFMAN

BANTAM BOOKS
NEW YORK · TORONTO · LONDON · SYDNEY · AUCKLAND

TEASE ME

A Bantam Book / July 1998

LOVESWEPT *and the wave design are registered trademarks of*
Bantam Books, *a division of* Bantam Doubleday Dell Publishing Group,
Inc. *Registered in U.S. Patent and Trademark Office and elsewhere.*

ISBN 0-553-44698-3

Published simultaneously in the United States and Canada

Bantam Books *are published by* Bantam Books, *a division of* Bantam Doubleday Dell Publishing Group, Inc. *Its trademark, consisting of the words*
"Bantam Books" *and the portrayal of a rooster, is Registered in U.S. Patent*
and Trademark Office and in other countries. Marca Registrada. Bantam
Books, *1540 Broadway, New York, New York 10036.*

To my editor,
Susann Brailey

For laughing in all
the right places

PROLOGUE

Tucker Morgan groaned in deep satisfaction as strong fingers worked down his bare back. "With your hands, Steph, you could achieve world peace. One body at a time." The only response was a short grunt, but then Steph didn't speak much English. "I think I'm in love."

There was a light tap on the door. The hands stopped. Tucker's moan wasn't one of delight. "Yes?" He felt the tension creep back into his neck.

"Sauna is ready for you, sir. Private, as you requested."

Tucker smiled and laid his head back down on the table. "Thank you." Ask and ye shall receive. He could get used to that. It was amazing what a difference a few more zeroes on the bottom of his bank balance made.

Steph resumed the deep massage on Tucker's lower back. The last time he'd had a massage, it had been administered with more enthusiasm than skill by a young woman while he was on assignment in Singapore. He let his eyes drift shut with a dreamy smile.

His job as head of an international security agency

had taken him to some of the world's most exotic ports of call. But, being a hands-on sort of boss, he'd spent most of his time sitting in hallways outside of posh suites, coordinating exit and entrance strategies, while dining on gourmet leftovers or vending-machine delicacies. And that was only when he wasn't prowling the grounds, typically at two A.M. during a rainstorm, making sure that there were no lunatics planning to step in and burst the surreal bubble of luxury that surrounded his latest jet-setting client.

A short slap brought him back to the present.

Tucker sat up and pulled a warm white towel around his hips before sliding off the table. He smiled at the two-hundred-and-fifty-pound Swede. "You're no Yuan Li, Stephan, but you give one helluva rubdown."

The masseur simply nodded and left the room. How much simpler his job would have been, Tucker thought wryly, if his clients had adopted Stephan's level of involvement with his customers.

Tucker exited through a back door that led directly into the men's locker room at the Fairmont Hotel spa and located the saunas. His name was listed in neat, hand-inked script next to number six.

Grinning, he entered his very own surreal luxury bubble and closed the door behind him, then sank down on the cedar bench. No more sitting on the outside, he thought. He picked up a small stoneware pitcher and poured a bit of water on the rocks piled in the center of the room. Sizzling vapor filled the air as he stretched out and rested his head on his arms.

Yep. This was what he wanted, what he'd sold his business for. He smiled to himself, recalling the overseas phone call and the long pause when he'd shocked Gunter

Lansdorf by responding with a yes to his umpteenth request to buy out Morgan & Manson Securities. Timing was everything.

Time. Time for himself. No one to worry about, answer to, plan for, think about, protect. It was no longer him taking care of them. He *was* a them. He took a deep breath and let it out slowly. Yes, it was good to be a them.

He must have drifted off, because the next thing he knew, someone was touching his back. He was dreaming. The smell of perfume wafted over him. Ah, a good dream. Fingers loosened the edge of his towel. Oh, this was going to be a great dream.

Then came a solid, stinging slap to his backside.

"Hey!" Grabbing his towel, Tucker rolled to a sitting position, whistling in a breath when the steamy bench came into contact with his newly steaming anatomy. "What in the hell—" Peering through the mist, he saw a short woman standing in front of him. His mouth dropped open.

He wasn't sure, but there had to be a law somewhere against seeing any relative over the age of seventy in nothing more than a small white towel.

"Aunt Lillian?"

"In the flesh."

Tucker glanced down. In the considerable flesh.

She smiled, reading his thoughts. One of her many irritating qualities. "And it's damn good flesh too." She primped at the painfully purple satin turban she'd woven snugly around her head. "Should be, I paid good money for it. Dr. Haarhuis and Sven the Destroyer are very happy men because of this body."

"I bet they are," he muttered. When she arched a

perfectly sculpted, penciled-on brow, he quickly said, "Sven the Destroyer?"

"My personal trainer. He used to be the pride of the World Wrestling Federation. Well, until that unfortunate incident with Magnificent Mongo." She extended her heavily beringed fingers and studied her matching painfully purple polish, then shot him a fast grin. "Ah, well, the WWF's loss was my gain."

"This is the men's locker room, Lillian. How did you get in here?"

"I'm old, my eyesight isn't what it used to be."

"Buzzards have worse eyesight than you."

"It took me all morning to track you down. Aren't you glad to see me?"

"If I saw any more of you, I'm pretty sure one of us could be arrested."

He still wasn't up to Lillian Parker speed, which fell somewhere between light and warp—or warped as the case may be—and he didn't move fast enough to avoid her firm pinch of the skin above his towel. He yelped—which made him feel like a very unmanly eight-year-old—and grabbed at the edge of his towel.

"A little soft around the middle." She gave him a quick once-over. "The big four-oh is staring you between the eyes, Tucker. Now is not the time to slack off."

He didn't tell her he'd been thinking the same thing. Which was why he'd signed up for an early-morning torture session with the Fairmont tennis pro before his appointment with Stephan.

"Nice buns, though," she added with a wink.

He'd missed her more than he realized. He flexed his arms in an exaggerated bodybuilding pose and with a bad Austrian accent said, "I might not give Sven a run for his money, but I still got it." He grinned at her. "And not a scalpel mark on me."

"Watch it, sonny," she warned, pointing a well-honed purple claw at him. "It may have been a few years since I've swatted that hard butt of yours, but you're still not too old to take a belt to."

"Gee, Aunt Lil, don't you think this has gotten kinky enough?"

She grinned. "Enough with the auntie stuff. You're making me feel old."

"Never happen." Lillian wasn't actually related to him. She'd been his mother's closest friend, and after Tucker's mother died when he was eight, she'd become his salvation. "You're family, Lillian." He smiled with true affection. "And for better or worse, you're all I've got."

Lillian sat down, wrapped an arm around him, and squeezed. He tried not to flinch. "What has Sven got you eating, anyway?"

She laughed. "Welcome back, Tucker. I kept expecting another one of those plane tickets you're so fond of sending. I'm getting too old to go traipsing around the world to see you. It's about time you came home. I actually missed you this time."

"Thanks, I think. And you can't be too old because you're ageless, remember? You've told me so enough times." It *had* been too long, though. He'd kept in contact by phone and flown her out to meet him for semiannual vacations, but he hadn't found the time to come back to Florida in . . . "Eight years," he said softly. He took in a slow breath. Guilt crept in with it. "Has it really been that long?"

"Yep. It was almost seven the time before that." Then she slapped his thigh hard enough to leave a mark and said, "But you got here just in time. I'm in need of your services."

"I sold Morgan & Manson Securities, Lillian."

She waved her hand. "Yes, yes, I got your letter. And how long were you going to wait to visit me?"

He eyed her warily. "Apparently not long enough."

"Hmm. Not really worried about your inheritance, are you?"

"What inheritance? You've always said you wouldn't leave one red cent when you go, and I'm holding you to it." He gave her a quick squeeze. "I was going to call you later this morning. I just got down here last night. What sort of trouble are you in this time? Speeding tickets piling up? Is old Sheriff Tumbleweed trying to put you in the slammer again, Leadfoot?"

"Roscoe Tumble wouldn't dream of trying to bring me up on some trumped-up reckless-driving charge. Besides, that floral landscape arrangement in the town circle was ugly, anyway."

Tucker wagged his finger. "We've talked about this before. Are you still driving that little red Miata? Remember what I said about a low profile?"

She waved away his concern. "This isn't about my driving record. I need you to do some investigative work for me."

"I'm not a detective, Aunt Lil. If you really need help, I can give you some names—"

"You're the closest I've got, Tucker. I can't trust this to someone I don't know."

She was dead serious. He covered her hand with his,

instantly concerned. "What's wrong? Are you really in some kind of trouble?"

"No, not me. It's Minerva. And two of my ladies. I think they might have gotten involved in something . . ." She lowered her voice. "Shady."

Her ladies, he knew, was how she referred to her clients at A Cut Above, the hair salon and minispa she'd owned and managed for the last seven years in the nearby retirement village of Sunset Shores. Minerva Cooper owned the café next door and was Lillian's best friend.

He relaxed. Minerva was about the same age as Lillian, seventy-two. And the average age of her clientele was about eighty. How much trouble could they be in? "I have some very reliable, discreet contacts who would be more than will—"

She shook her head. "No. It has to be you. I could be wrong about this, and I need some proof before I decide how to handle it. I'm not involving some stranger."

"What exactly do you think they've done?"

She leaned closer and whispered, "About a month ago I went out back to throw some boxes away and I saw Minerva, along with Bernice Henshaw and Betty Louise Strickmeyer, talking to this . . . man."

"We're alone, Lillian. You don't have to whisper. What was so suspicious about the guy?"

"He was young—"

"How young? Late twenties, early thirties? Older than a college kid, younger than you?"

She ignored his scowl. "He had long hair slicked back into a ponytail. He was dressed nicely enough: pleated pants, nice shirt, tie, but it was all in black."

"It's not a crime to wear black, Lillian. Even in Florida. Stupid maybe, sweaty certainly."

Lillian glared at him. "There was something about him. I can't put my finger on it. He wasn't . . . normal."

"Normal compared to what?"

She swatted him. "And he was rather animated."

Tucker rubbed his shoulder. "Angry?"

"Well, no. More like excited, but not happy excited. I couldn't see the ladies' faces. But I'm telling you it was strange. I know everyone around Sunset Shores, but I'd never seen him before. And they were talking in the alley as if it was a secret."

"Have you talked to them about it?"

"Heavens, no! I didn't want them to think I was snooping."

He looked at her.

She huffed. "Okay, so I did poke around a bit. I didn't want to embarrass them or anything, so I asked a few leading questions, gave them a few openings, but they never mentioned him or anything else unusual. Not even Minerva."

Which had obviously hurt Lillian's feelings. He squeezed her hand. "Maybe he was lost and asking for directions."

"That doesn't explain why they were all out there in the first place. Minerva had reason to be behind her café. But what were Bernice and Betty Louise doing back there?"

"I'm sure there is a simple explanation. One chance meeting with a strange character doesn't mean they're involved in—"

"I'm not some silly, senile old woman, Tucker. I know what I saw. And it wasn't only that one meeting. There was another incident."

He swallowed a sigh. She was serious about this. "Another 'incident'?"

"I decided to talk to Minerva's niece, Lainey. You know, I told you about her. She moved down here about two years ago to help poor Minerva out when she got pneumonia. When her aunt got better, Lainey decided to stay on. Not that I blame her. She'd just gone through a real nasty divorce. Oh, the mess she left back in Philly." Lillian whistled. "I tell you, from what Minerva told me, that ex-husband of hers, Conrad, was a real spineless toad. Couldn't even stand up to his own mother. And did I tell you about the mother?" She rolled her eyes. "Well, you would not believe—"

"Whoa, whoa. Let's get back to the 'incident.' "

Lillian frowned. Tucker knew she hated to have good gossip interrupted. "If you'd visit more often, you'd be more up-to-date on this stuff. I—"

"Lillian."

She glared at him. "Okay, okay. Anyway, as I was saying, I couldn't put it out of my mind, so I decided to talk with Lainey, but I didn't want Minerva to know. I know Lainey goes to Big Sam's early on Saturday to get something for the fish special, so I met her there. Or I would have. I was getting out of my car when I saw her across the street." She smacked his leg for emphasis. "She was talking to the same man!"

He rubbed his thigh. "Are you sure?"

"Of course I'm sure. Ol' buzzard eyes, remember?"

He didn't bother trying to look repentant.

"And they were arguing."

"Did you confront her about it?"

"Didn't get the chance. She was obviously upset, but

he didn't seem to care. He said something to her, then walked off. Before I could get to her, she jumped into her car and left. This was last week. I've been too busy to get her alone again."

Tucker still wasn't all that concerned, but it was obvious that Lillian was. "Did you tell anyone else about this?"

"No. If the grapevine here got their hands on a satellite, they could put CNN out of business. Word would get out one way or another, and that's the last thing I want. I wouldn't want to put any of them in danger. Someone could get hurt."

"No one is going to get hurt. There isn't any danger—"

"We won't know that for sure until I get more information." She somehow managed to look up at him and yet down her nose at the same time. "And don't tell me you don't have the time to help." She sighed and made that annoying tsking sound. "Forty years old and jobless. You should thank me. I'm doing you a favor."

"Thirty-nine. And I'm hardly hurting. The sale on MMSI was finalized barely a week ago. I'm on vacation."

"And then what?"

He'd been afraid she'd ask that. But this was not the time to explain how deeply affected he'd been by his business partner and friend Peter Manson's tragically early death. How Tucker had looked in the mirror the morning after Pete's funeral and seen an almost-forty-year-old man who was heading in the same direction. Life had somehow passed him by. Like Pete, work had become his life. There was no wife—trophy, ex, or otherwise—no children of any decimal percentage, no oversized dog to dig holes in the yard he also didn't have. He needed a new life. He needed a life, period.

Lansdorf had called later that morning and offered him an out. With no plan, no parachute, he'd taken the offer, and he hadn't regretted it. He looked at Lillian's determined face. Not yet, anyway.

"This won't take more than a week or two," she said.

"Lillian—"

"A little undercover work."

His eyebrows narrowed. "Undercover?"

Her eyes brightened. "It hit me when I ran into that gorgeous young masseur while I was trying to find you. Stephan, I believe he said his name was. Those Swedes have such incredible blue eyes. . . ." Her eyes started to glaze over.

"Lillian?" He snapped his fingers.

She looked at him with a smile that made him nervous. "It's really the perfect idea. No one at the shop knows you. They might question your name since I have been known to talk about you, but I can deal with that. Of course, you could always be Lance or something."

Lance? Tucker closed his eyes and counted to ten.

Lillian gave him a small punch in the shoulder. "Stop worrying. I have it all figured out."

Tucker rubbed his arm, thinking quickly. But any last-ditch evasive maneuvers died on the planning table when she added, "You said yourself that I'm the only family you've got. Surely you can do me this one small favor."

He felt eight years old again. She'd been there for him then, when no one else had. The childhood summers he'd spent with her in Florida after his mom died had been his salvation. There might not be a blood tie between them, but she was the only family he had. And she'd never asked him for a single thing.

Still . . . Undercover in a beauty shop? A beauty shop for blue hairs? He sighed. It was only for a week or two.

"Yes, Aunt Lillian."

ONE

At the jingle of the tiny door bells, Madelaine Cooper looked up from the counter, where she was cutting the day's pie special, key lime, into narrow slices. She smiled as two of Aunt Minnie's Wednesday-morning regulars came through the door. "Hello, Irma. Hi, Ida." She made a kissing noise at the miniature pinscher peeking his black, pointy-eared head out from Ida's oversized purse. "And good morning to you, Mr. Maxwell."

Instead of receiving the usual chorus of friendly hellos and a yip from Mr. Max on the way to "their" table, the identical twin sisters rushed to the counter. "Rushed" was a relative term. At eighty-two they wouldn't set any land-speed records.

Always the competitive one, Irma hit the linoleum counter first. Rapping it with the handle of her cane, she announced, "Lainey, you won't believe what Lillian has gone and done."

Ida ambled up, slightly out of breath. "Came out first and has never waited for me since."

"Zip it, Ida. I let you get combed out first this morning, didn't I?"

Ida patted her steel-blue helmet of hair. "Yes, but only because you wanted to grill that poor, sweet shampoo girl, Lisette, on the new masseur."

Irma harrumphed. It was a sound Lainey hadn't really thought possible until she'd met the older-by-one-full-minute Armbruster sister. Irma glared at Ida. "*I* wanted to tell her."

Ida suddenly discovered that Mr. Maxwell needed a loving pat and a treat from her pocketbook. But Lainey didn't miss the small, victorious smile.

Lainey swallowed her own smile when she caught Irma glaring at her. "So Lillian finally found a new masseuse? Have you made an appointment yet? I know how much you both adored your sessions with Helga."

Ida sighed in reverence. "My, yes. She was wonderful."

"That's just it," Irma put in. "It's not a Helga."

The Scandinavian woman had been gone for close to a year, but the ladies still talked about her departure as if it had happened yesterday. It had been all the scandal when she'd run off with Hector Wadlow, the newly widowed owner of Wadlow's Hardware. Hector's wife had been a steady client of Helga's, which had naturally led to detailed speculation over what exactly had caused poor Mrs. Wadlow's heart attack. And, before any of them could grill him properly, Hector had sold his business and hightailed it off to Europe with Helga, crushing the local ladies, who'd lost both a masseuse and a fresh bachelor in one cruel blow.

Lainey went back to slicing the pie. "I thought Lillian had given up trying to replace her."

"Well, this one might make it," Ida said, still patting Mr. Maxwell.

Irma rapped the counter again. "That's why we're here."

Lainey jumped, then carefully placed her knife on the counter. "You're not here for your morning coffee and pie?"

Irma snorted. She was good with noises. "No time for that. We want you to—"

"Not *we*, Irma, you," Ida corrected. "*I* wanted nothing to do with your scheme. *I* said we should leave the situation alone."

"Situation?" Lainey looked to Irma. "Scheme?"

"*We*"—she shot a challenging look at Ida, who immediately began digging in her purse for another doggie treat—"think you should make an appointment. At Lillian's."

Ida cupped a hand to her mouth and leaned closer. "For a massage." For all her apparent disapproval, there was no missing the gleam of excitement in her faded gray eyes.

What were they up to? Lainey waited for an explanation, but they both stared at her with hopeful looks on their faces. "A massage? But I don't need—"

Irma grabbed her wrist with surprising strength. "Yes. You do."

"You're the only one we can trust," Ida added earnestly.

"Working so hard, standing all day. It'll do you good," Irma went on.

"But why—" Lainey broke off as understanding dawned. "Oh, you want me to test her out."

In the two years since she'd moved to the small Gulf

Coast community, Lainey had gotten to know most of the Sunset Shores residents. Minerva's Café was the only local nonfast-food place that served breakfast and lunch and had long ago become a local gathering spot. She knew that none of the residents were hurting financially, but most were still on some sort of fixed income. If it would make the sisters feel more comfortable to have a personal recommendation before making their own appointments, well, Lainey could swing one massage.

She went over her schedule. She had to run several errands the following afternoon since the café was catering several luncheons at the senior center the next week. On Fridays she was always swamped, and Minerva had her club meeting that afternoon. "Maybe I can squeeze something in on Saturday."

"Nothing sooner?" Irma demanded.

"Irma!" Ida smiled at Lainey. "That will be fine. Thank you, sweetie." She patted her hand. "You're a good girl."

"But, Ida, we can't wait that long," Irma whispered in a low hiss. "She'll certainly find out by—"

Something was definitely up, but Lainey was at a loss to pinpoint it. Curious but not worried, she smiled with true affection at both sisters. Squabbling aside, they were sweet and truly cared about her. Lainey jumped into the fray. The twins could make a week-long event out of arguing over their soup selection. "I'm sorry I can't make it any sooner."

"You're sure?"

"Stop badgering the poor girl, Irma," Ida chided. "She agreed, after all." She moved closer to her sister and lowered her voice. "We really should tell her though."

Irma quickly leaned past her. "Thank you so much,

Lainey, we knew we could count on you. Minerva is right to be so proud of you." She turned to Ida. "Come on, I want to check out that dress down at Natties."

"But . . ." Ida took several steps behind Irma, then turned and shot Lainey an apologetic look. "We'll drop in for lunch Saturday."

"But you have bridge on Sat—" Lainey didn't bother finishing her sentence. They were gone. Now what was all that about? They hadn't even stayed for coffee. She shrugged, but before she got busy and forgot, she dialed Lillian's and reserved an early-morning slot. Lillian's receptionist, Jewel, was harried with the early-morning rush but seemed both surprised and happy at the appointment request.

Saturday morning at eight-thirty, thirty-four-year-old Lainey Cooper was getting her first massage. Hey, she thought with a smile of anticipation, it was the least she could do to help out some friends. Before she'd left Philly, both Conrad, her ex-husband, and his mother, Agatha Maitland of the Philadelphia Maitlands, which was how she always thought of her, had warned her that living in a retirement village would be a stifling bore. As if living with them had been a riot-a-minute, she thought dryly.

Well, they hadn't met the Armbruster sisters. Imagining Irma and Ida at one of her ex-mother-in-law's stiff-necked, pinkie-extended, Junior League teas had Lainey laughing as she went back to slicing the pie.

"I did not sell a successful international business so that I could spend my days rubbing down eighty-year-old bodies." Tucker frowned down at Lillian's bent head. Her white-gold hair had been ruthlessly combed into a deceptively wispy, gravity-defying cloud that was held together with enough spray cement to make it hurricane-proof. The head beneath it was every bit as hard.

"You sold an international business because you're having a midlife crisis. I'm offering you decent work. Stop whining."

Lillian was wearing purple leggings under a long, silky tropical shirt printed with eyestraining pink, purple, and white flowers. They perfectly matched the ones sprouting from the middle straps of her wedge-heeled, white patent-leather sandals, not to mention the ones clipped onto her ears and painted on her purple nails. Tucker had taken one look at her and wished for the towel and satin turban.

She lifted the glasses that hung around her neck on a long chain of plastic pearls, slid them on halfway down her nose, then went back to surveying her product invoice sheet. "How many Exo Waves do I have?"

From his perch on a footstool, Tucker scanned the top shelf of supplies. "Six. I could crack ribs, Lillian. Hell, one wrong move, and their entire skeleton might disintegrate." He turned to face her. "I don't know what I'm doing."

She shoved the clipboard at him. "You're helping me with inventory and having a tantrum. Trade places."

"I don't have tantrums." He tightened his lower lip and dutifully stepped off the stool.

"It's the one job here you can do, and the added benefit to it is that it must be done privately, where you have the best shot of gaining confidences and getting some inside information. Heaven knows the things they used to tell Helga. Of course, she didn't understand much English, but—"

"Lillian."

"My ladies are a lot tougher than they look, Tucker. If Helga didn't send them to the ER, you certainly won't."

"I'm not so sure about that. And do you really think they'll trust a man?"

She eyed him over her glasses. "Well, that's a loaded question women have been grappling with for eons." She turned back to counting perms, ignoring his scowl. "You're charming. When you want to be. And good-looking. For your age."

"Please stop before my ego gets too big." He switched tactics. "Don't you need a license for this sort of thing? You could get sued or worse."

"I'm not advertising that you have one, but I won't lie if asked, which I won't be. They'll be clamoring for you, trust me. And this will all be over before the state board catches on. You did read the books and watch the videos I got you, right?"

"I hardly think *Shiatsu: The Sensual Way to Rub Your Mate the Right Way* is part of any accreditation course on clinical massage."

"Oh, don't be such a snob. I happen to think it was wonderful. Why, last weekend, I lit a few candles and invited that nice Stanley Shemanski over and we—"

"Stop right there." He knew when he was whipped. "You win. I hope your insurance premiums are up-to-date."

"Let me worry about that. You worry about finding out what Minerva, Bernice, and Betty Louise have gotten themselves mixed up in." She reached out and pushed his bottom lip in. "Buck up. It won't take that long."

He wasn't so sure about that. "It might take longer than you think to gain their confidence. If Louise Betty, Bernice, and Minerva aren't talking about—"

"Betty Louise. And keep your voice down. The walls have hearing aids around here."

"I still think that if you're that worried about them, you could ask the sheriff to help."

"I couldn't go to Roscoe. He's a friend. The ladies would be mortified if—"

"It's his job, Lillian." But he didn't push it. She'd been quite adamant about not involving Old Tumbleweed. He hadn't been any more successful in changing her mind about hiring a real investigator.

Lillian leaned closer. "I did think of a lead."

Tucker worked at not rolling his eyes. "A lead?"

"Bernice's husband, Leland, God rest his soul, was quite the gambler. He loved the dogs. Did pretty well, too, as I recall. Maybe Bernice has hit the tracks. Maybe she got in over her head with a bookie." She frowned. "Betty Louise is a mouse and would do anything Bernice told her to, but Minerva . . ." She shook her head. "That I can't figure out. Other than bingo, she's not much of a gambler. Besides, she's a cat person."

Tucker massaged his temple.

She waved a dismissive hand. "Anyhow, this is a lead worth pursuing. I think they're involved in something, and they've somehow gotten in over their heads. They'd be too embarrassed to tell anyone. But I'm afraid they're in danger. I tell you, that guy looked menacing. He's certainly not from around here."

"Anyone under seventy is not from around here."

Ignoring him, Lillian did a last scan of the shelves,

then snapped the cupboard shut, slipped her glasses off, and turned back to him. "You'll do fine."

"What makes you think they're going to open up and spill their guts to me?"

She laughed. "Don't kid yourself. You are underestimating the effect of strong male hands on a naked female body. Some of these women haven't had a man's hands on them in over a decade."

Tucker groaned silently, and his stomach tied into another knot.

"Stop worrying. Follow the videotape, sans the candles and Bolero music, and they'll be eating out of your hands."

"Very funny."

Lillian gave him a sharp once-over. "Actually, I'm more worried about heart attacks than cracked ribs."

"Oh, so now the over-the-hill guy is okay?"

"Hey, if you're single and breathing on your own, you're not over the hill to them."

Tucker was saved from a reply when the intercom crackled. "Tucker, your eight-thirty is here."

His what? *Oh, no.* A client. He had a client. He looked at Lillian with unconcealed dread. "I have an eight-thirty?"

Blue eyes twinkling, she said, "Looks like it." She shoved at his shoulder, almost pushing him out of the small room. "Go on." He tried to stop, but she swatted him with her clipboard.

"Hey!" He rubbed his backside but moved down the hallway.

"And Tucker?"

He glared at her. "What?"

"Knock 'em dead, honey."

"Not funny." He swore under his breath. What in the hell had he gotten himself into? He wondered if he shouldn't have argued so hard to use his own name. But Lance? He still shuddered. "And I changed my mind about that inheritance," he called back. Her only response was a laugh.

Lainey tucked in the towel more firmly above her breasts and tried to find a graceful, minimum-exposure way to climb onto the massage table. The room was warm and softly lit, the exotic fragrance of heated oils mixing with the soft jazz being piped in to create a relaxing atmosphere. It was not at all the clinical setup she'd imagined. She laughed at herself. She was there to be pampered, not probed. If she could get over feeling so exposed, she might actually enjoy herself.

Ignoring the fact that in minutes she would be even more exposed, she gripped the knot at the top of her coral-pink towel, flattened her other palm along the end that barely dangled past her backside, and sidled over to the side of the linen-covered table. No footstool. Hmmm.

That made graceful and minimum exposure an either/or proposition. What she needed was leverage. She tightened her grip on both ends of her towel and looked at the hip-high padded table. "I'm short one hand."

"You can use one of mine," a deep voice suggested helpfully.

With a muffled shriek, she spun around. The tall man standing inside the doorway was dressed in white pleated pants and a white crewneck T-shirt. He had thick, finger-ruffled, dark blond hair and blue eyes that would make even Mel Gibson's wife drool. The first thing that struck her was that Irma was most certainly right. He was definitely no Helga.

The second thing that hit her was the real reason the sisters had conspired to get her in there.

"Matchmakers," she muttered. She thought the Charlie Kovacs incident had cured the Armbruster sisters of their matchmaking tendencies. Charlie was the "nice young accountant" who gave tax seminars at the senior center whom she had agreed to go out with. She'd firmly believed that if she hadn't said yes, the sisters might have come up with someone a lot worse than a short, balding CPA.

As it turned out, Charlie had been quite charming, and she'd continued to see him. He'd been confident without being overbearing and had no mother in sight, so Lainey had seen him as a safe way for her to reenter social life as a single woman. And he had been just that . . . right up until the day the risk-free tax shelter he'd gotten her into was exposed as a scam, which had resulted in her being audited and heavily penalized by the IRS and Charlie being sent to live in a nice minimum-security prison. They had all decided that in the "men" department, there couldn't be much worse than Charlie Kovacs.

Lainey looked at the broad-shouldered back and perfectly shaped butt of the man currently sliding a sign that said Occupied into a metal track on the outside of the door. He was a fantasy waiting to happen. And yet she knew with absolute certainty that somehow, some way, the Kovacs theory was about to be proven wrong. Good things did not happen to Madelaine Cooper.

"He's got to be married, gay, or a serial killer who likes to massage old people to death," she murmured.

He stepped into the room. "I'm sorry, what did you say?"

The instant she heard the soft click of the door closing, the room's temperature went from pleasantly warm to uncomfortably hot.

When she didn't answer right away, he said, "I didn't mean to startle you. I knocked. I must not have done it hard enough."

There wasn't anything this man couldn't do hard enough. The images that thought produced made her throat go dry. *Resist, Lainey. Be strong. Remember Charlie. Remember Conrad. And if that doesn't work, remember Conrad's mother.* She straightened as a vision of Agatha's disapproving glare swam across her mind. "I don't guess you're the towel guy or the shampoo, uh, boy."

He grinned. "I'm Tucker, your masseur. And I can't tell you how relieved—uh, happy I am to see you." When she clutched her towel, he glanced down, then quickly back up. "Uh, not *see*-you you see you. To serve you, I mean." Realizing he wasn't making matters better, he gave up and shrugged far too endearingly. He stepped forward and stuck out his hand. "Tucker Morgan, pleased to meet you."

Lainey could have sworn her kneecaps liquefied. She pressed against the table for support. "Pleased to meet you too." Too pleased, judging by the happy hula her hormones were doing at the moment. Her gaze moved to his hand. It was wide and tanned, with long fingers that looked entirely too capable. And in less than a few minutes they would be running all over her body.

Her oiled, naked body.

She tried shallow breathing. It didn't help much. Even Agatha's nightmarish visage deserted her. Not even for the twins could she do this. No matter her good intentions, it *had* been a long time since Charlie. He'd start rubbing, she'd start groaning, he'd slide his hands lower . . . No, uh-uh. She'd never done this before, but she was fairly certain writhing was not acceptable behavior during a massage. And it was a moot point anyway, since there was no way she'd attempt a graceful table mount now.

"I, uh—" She broke off at the hoarse sound of her voice, took a stabilizing breath, then clutched the towel tighter when it began to slide. "Listen, it's like this. I'm sure you're wonderful—"

He let his hand drop back to his side. "Actually, I'm nervous as hell. This is my first day. You're my first client."

He was nervous? Oh, wonderful. "I'm your first?" Why did saying that make her skin all shivery? *No, no, you don't, Lainey.* Sternly ignoring her hormones, which were too busy planning a major party in her lower extremities to listen to her anyway, she firmed her spine and her resolve. "Don't take it personally. It's nothing you said or did, but I really don't think I want a massage after all."

He looked . . . relieved. Not upset or offended. Relieved. It should have made her feel better. It didn't. In fact, it made her feel . . . rebellious. Defiant.

Stop right now, she told herself. This was the exact moment when she needed to take control and think clearly, not throw caution to the wind. If there was an Olympic event for caution throwing, she'd be a repeat gold medal winner. Among other things, it had gotten her married, divorced, audited, and almost jailed. It was about to get her massaged.

He started to turn back to the door. *Don't do it, Lainey.*

Too late. He'd all but dared her. The parts of her that were on hormone cruise control cheered her on. "Since I'm here, though, what the heck." He swung back, his expression a mix of surprise and dread. It was the sting of the dread part that made her let go of the bottom end of her towel and strong-arm herself up onto the side of the table. That went so well, she crossed her legs and said, "You'll be my first too."

TWO

Tucker cleared his throat and crossed the room, skirting the table—and his client—on his way to the neatly arranged cart positioned at the opposite end. He kept his eyes trained on the bottles of lotion . . . and off her legs. Legs he would soon be rubbing hot oil onto.

He wasn't crazy about the Mr. Clean uniform Lillian had insisted he wear, but at least it had pleated pants. He didn't have to be a professional to know that a masseur wasn't supposed to be rock hard while working. Of course, the guy in Lillian's video might be the exception to the rule, but then he hadn't been looking to get paid. Tucker stifled a groan.

He grabbed a bottle of oil. "Why don't you go ahead and lie down."

She started to lean back. "On your stomach," he added quickly. He turned his back to her. "Let me know when you're ready."

He listened as she settled herself, trying in vain not to picture the procedure.

"All set."

Bracing himself, he turned. The only mercy he received was that her head was pillowed on her arms, facing away from him. The rest of her was displayed in all its hardly terry-cloth-covered curvy glory. The towel dipped neatly against the back of her thighs, emphasizing the sweet curve of her backside. The top edge stopped just above her ribs, displaying the smooth skin of her back and shoulders that had been exposed to the sun just enough to look as if it had been dipped in honey.

Some of the warm oil oozed out in his hand. He swallowed another groan and relaxed his grip on the squeeze bottle. Her hair was pinned up in a pile of warm brown curls; the soft lighting reflected gentle golden highlights that he doubted were the result of any of Lillian's capable staff. His fingers tightened against the urge to reach out and slide the pins from her hair to satisfy his sudden need to discover what those silky waves would look like spread over her slender neck and shoulders.

She chose that moment to turn her head toward him. "Is everything okay?" Her smile was dazzling.

He abruptly set the bottle down on the cart before he shot the warm, sticky contents all over her. The analogy wasn't lost on him.

"Absolutely," he said, pasting a bright smile on his face. He reached beneath the table for a white linen drape and snapped it out over her, covering her from mid-thigh to mid-back.

She laid her head back down, facing away from him again. "I can't believe I'm doing this."

Tucker's grin eased into something a bit more natural. Neither can I, he thought. At least not professionally.

"Any back or neck problems I should be aware of?" he asked, feeling a bit more relaxed. Something in her tone, a trace of her earlier uncertainty maybe, restored a bit of his control.

"Nope, fit as a fiddle."

She sure looked that way to him, he thought silently. He grabbed the bottle, squeezed some oil on his hands, and worked it into his palms. This was just a job. He should consider himself a lucky son of a gun to have a young body with solid bones to practice on, and get this over with. Recalling the video instructions—after all, Shiatsu was Shiatsu, wasn't it?—he reached for her shoulders.

"Do you need to take the towel off?" she asked without turning.

His hands froze an inch from her skin. "Ah, well, seeing as this is your first time and all, I didn't want you to feel uncomfortable."

"Well, this does feel a little weird," she added, sounding relieved. "But I'm not as uncomfortable as I thought I'd be." She let out a small laugh. "I guess you have a good tableside manner. No need for silly modesty, right? After all, you are a professional."

Tucker swallowed hard. *If you only knew.*

"I'll just close my eyes and put myself into your capable hands."

That did it. He pulled his capable hands away. He couldn't go through with this. No matter what he told himself—or her—he was not a professional, and even if he could fake that on a functional level, he sure as hell wasn't going to be able to on a personal one.

"Listen, maybe we should—"

"No, really, just slide it out. I mean, the sheet stays on, right?"

"Right," he said, then cleared the roughness from his

throat. What the hell. He reached for the towel. "Lift up a bit." She did. He loosened the back of the towel and slid it off, being careful to keep the linen sheet pinned to the table with his free hand.

"And don't worry," she said earnestly as she settled her head back on her arms. "I know you're probably a bit nervous with this being your first day, but I've never had one of these, so I won't know if you're doing anything wrong, anyway."

He looked at her semidraped body. The way the sheet clung to her every curve, the stark contrast between white linen and smooth golden skin, the hint of soft breasts pressed against the table . . .

Professional wasn't even on the list of what he was feeling at the moment.

This is ridiculous, he scolded himself. He'd protected some of the most gorgeous women on the planet and shared various intimacies with a fair number of others—many who hadn't even spoken his language—and at no time had he ever felt so rattled by a woman.

He could blame it on lack of female companionship of any kind of late. What with the funeral and all of the life-changing decisions that had resulted from Pete's death, he hadn't been too interested. He hadn't really planned to be for a while, not until he sorted a few things out.

There was no denying he was interested now, however. In what, though? That was the question he hadn't answered. And he wouldn't. Now was not the time, no matter the opportunity.

With renewed concentration on the purpose literally at hand, he straightened the linen sheet and began to work on her shoulders. Just because the soft feel of supple muscles going pliant beneath his fingertips made his entire body tighten did not mean he wasn't focused on his one and only goal, which was to get through this appointment, then track down Lillian and convince her that there had to be another way to get her information.

Conversation. Distraction. "So what made you decide to get a massage?" he asked genially. "Special occasion?"

"Actually, it was the twins' idea."

Tucker's fingers faltered for a moment, then continued working the sides of her neck. *Twins?* Tucker gave a rueful silent laugh. There he was, drooling like a pimply adolescent over this woman, and she was a happily married mother of twin tots. *You really do need a break, Morgan.* Seeing as she was probably somewhere in her late twenties, early thirties, it was more likely Dad had arranged this little gift. He wondered if Dad was the jealous type. He sincerely hoped not, then felt even more the fraud. He was deceiving an entire family.

"And it falls more under the heading of busybody than anything else," she said, her voice going all soft as he absently worked his way down her back.

His mind was still on the happy family giving Mom a nice break only to have her groped by a guy posing as a masseur in some silly scheme of Lillian's. This was definitely beginning and ending right there. As soon as he was done.

After all, they'd paid for a massage for Mom, and she was going to go out of there satisfied, even if it meant he had to spend the three hours directly afterward in a cold shower. He massaged more deeply.

"I think I'll have to forgive them this time," she said, then let loose a long sigh that stretched his pleats no matter how businesslike he commanded his thoughts to be.

"So what made you decide to become a masseur?" she asked, her voice deeper, almost drowsy. "Were you in sports or something? You seem like a pretty fit guy."

"I'm, uh, doing it as a favor. For Lillian. She was a close friend of my mother's." It was bad enough that he was deceiving her about his credentials. He was determined not to lie any more than he had to.

"That's really nice of you. I guess you've heard all about Helga then."

Helga? It took him a moment but he placed the name. "Oh, Helga, yes. The former masseuse."

"No one has been able to take her place."

"I understand she was quite popular. But I'm only here temporarily."

She started to lift up and turn her head, presumably to look at him, but he pressed her gently but firmly back to the table. "That's a shame," she said. "I think you'll gain quite a quick following here."

Not if I can help it. Before she could resume her line of questioning, Tucker turned the tables on her. "Are you a regular client here? I don't mean to sound surprised. It's just that I assumed all of Lillian's clients were Sunset Shores residents."

"I am a resident. I live next—" Her answer died out on a long groan as Tucker pressed his thumbs down and ran them along her spine, then worked back up to her shoulders in a slow, circular motion. "I'm beginning to think I owe Ida and Irma an apology," she said on a satisfied sigh.

Tucker's hands paused then quickly resumed. Ida and Irma? What kind of names were those for little kids? At least she'd distracted him from his body-hardening reaction. He felt as if he were on an amusement-park ride, which was whipping his body up and down, yanking his emotions from side to side.

"Family names?" he asked, then mentally kicked himself. He might be having a tough time, but she was coasting through this fine. He didn't need to rile her up by making her defend her kids' old-fashioned names. He shifted to the foot of the table.

"I never asked," she answered easily. "With them you're lucky to get a word in edgewise. I take it you haven't met them yet. They didn't waste any time finding out about you." She sighed again as he slowly began to manipulate her toes and the soles of her feet. "But even though I resent them for doing this, I have to say I will recommend you to them. You're really good, Mr. Morgan."

"Tucker," he said absently. She wanted him to massage her *children?* She seemed bright and intelligent, and it went without saying that she came wrapped up in a beautiful package, but she was also wacko. "Uh, I'm not sure," he started slowly, "but I don't think Lillian caters to the, uh, younger set."

"Younger set?" Sliding one hand up for balance, she lifted her head and looked over her shoulder at him. "What are you talking about?"

He was too far away at the base of the table to snag the slowly slipping linen sheet, but her confused expression captured his full attention, anyway. "Your children. The twins. I don't think we cater to children, here."

"My chil—" She broke off as understanding dawned in her eyes, and she started to laugh. The additional movement sent the linen sheet sliding south at an alarming rate. Tucker made a lunge for it at the same time that she realized the problem and jerked around, grabbing for it as well.

She came up with a handful of linen. He came up with a handful of . . . her. He barely had time to register the full, firm warmth of her breast and the way her nipple peaked against his palm before her gasp had him releasing her and turning his back.

"I'm—I apologize. Truly. I was just trying to keep the sheet from sliding to the—"

"It's okay, really," she said sincerely. But she sounded quite breathless.

Tucker kept his back to her.

"All wrapped up, you can turn around now."

Tucker turned to find her seated on the side of the table, the sheet wrapped fully around her like a sarong, covering her to the knees. Her hair had come down and now fell in soft waves above her shoulders. Her expression was sincere, but humor glinted in her dark green eyes.

"Well, at least this will have been a memorable first for both of us."

"I really am sorry—"

She raised one hand, then slapped it back to her chest when the sheet began to slip. "No problem," she said, her cheeks darkening a bit even as she laughed. "But there is one thing you should know. I'm not married." At his confused expression, she hurried to add, "What I mean is, I don't have twins. I don't have kids at all."

Tucker refused to consider why this news should elate him so much. "Then who are Ida and Irma?"

"Two of Lillian's clients. They're identical twins. They're also eighty-two."

Tucker ran a mental replay then chuckled as he

thought over their unknowing "who's on first" conversation. "You had me going there, you know."

She laughed too. "It wasn't intentional. It never occurred to me that you'd assume—"

He lifted a hand. "My fault. So," he said, seemingly unable to wipe the happy grin from his face, "they set you up, huh?"

He was pleased when she smiled at his teasing. "Sucker born every minute. I should know." She'd said it jokingly, but the edge of vulnerability made Tucker curious.

He filed his questions away for the time being. Right now there were more urgent things to find out, such as what her name was. "So how do you know the twins? Great-niece or great-granddaughter or something?"

"Oh, they're customers of mine. Well, my aunt Minerva's, really."

"You mean you're Minerva's niece? From the café next door?"

Her smile faded a bit as she studied his face. "One and the same. I'm Madelaine Cooper, but most people call me Lainey." She stuck out her hand, then snatched it back to catch the towel. "Sorry." Her cheeks pinkened again, but she gamely continued. "And despite the Armbruster sisters' shenanigans, I'm pleased to meet you, Tucker. Really. And don't worry, I won't say anything about . . . Well, what I mean is, I won't complain. After all," she continued with a nervous laugh, "it felt wonderful. I mean, you have great hands and— Oh, boy." She groaned and dipped her chin.

Amused and more intrigued than he thought he could be, he watched as she took a deep breath for composure and lifted her head again.

"I don't want to jeopardize your job," she said with admirable calm. "You really are good at this."

Tucker thought he heard a repressed sigh on that last part, but his mind was still on the fact that this was Minerva's niece and one of the few people who knew the mystery man. "I appreciate that," he said, almost absently, relieved that at least part of his brain was still on his real purpose for being there.

"Well," she said when the silence spun out. "I think I've had about all my system can take for one day."

Her gaze caught his suddenly. He didn't comment, but the brief flash of vulnerability in her eyes did bring him out of his musings. She was a fascinating mix of bold, beautiful, and shy. "Me too," he said with a grin that invited her to share the humor in the situation.

He wished he could share the entire story with her, was compelled to, anyway, despite Lillian's misgivings. If he did have to go through with this ridiculous charade, it would be good to have at least one person—besides Lillian—to be truthful with.

Given her obvious sense of humor, he was certain Lainey would find the whole thing as absurd as he did. It also occurred to him that telling her about it could clear up the entire matter. She might be able to explain away the entire situation. But something—his sixth sense or whatever you want to call it—stopped him at the last moment.

He could tell himself it was loyalty to Lillian and her concerns about handling her suspicions a certain way, but something else stopped him too.

He wanted to get to know Lainey a little better before he decided how to pursue the situation.

"Well," she said, "I'm sure you're busy. I'll let you get on with your other appointments."

"Actually, you're the only one I had today," he said, not knowing if it was true, but he could remedy that. "I don't suppose you're free for lunch? Or maybe a quick cup of coffee?"

His offer obviously surprised her. Apparently she wasn't as affected by the masseur as he was by his new client. His ego took the blow in stride. After all, it was information he was really after.

Yeah, okay, his little voice shot back.

"I'm afraid I can't," she said. "We're catering a luncheon later today, and I've got a ton of things to do. I really did this as a favor to the twins." Her eyes brightened a bit as a hint of her bolder side flashed through again in a short grin. "The things I endure for friendship."

Tucker smiled. "Mind if I stop in later for a cup of coffee?"

She shrugged, then grabbed at her drape again. "We never turn away a paying customer."

Tucker wondered at the wariness that had crept into her smile. It might be the natural reaction to a professional making a personal play for a client. He supposed it probably was unethical, if he was truly a professional— which he wasn't. He realized he was drawing a fine line, but it *was* a line.

"Lillian says Minerva's pot pie isn't to be missed. Maybe I'll stop in for lunch instead."

Looking relieved, she said, "I'm sure you won't be disappointed." She slid carefully from the table, her bare feet sinking into the plush carpeting a few feet from him.

The top of her head came to about his chin, forcing her to look up as she spoke.

"I'll be out on buying runs, so I'll miss you, but Aunt Minnie prides herself on her repeat customers, so we'll probably bump into each other again."

"I don't plan on being here very long, so I'd really like to—"

"I really have to get going," she said apologetically. She backed toward the door. "Thanks again." She twisted the knob and slipped out before he could do anything to prevent it.

Tucker stood there for several seconds, mulling over his disappointment, dealing with the fact that it had little to do with solving Lillian's mystery and a whole lot to do with one Madalaine Cooper. Then another snippet of Lillian's initial conversation sprang to mind. He snapped his fingers. "Today's Saturday." He grinned. Lillian wouldn't be too happy about losing her masseur on a busy Saturday, but he hoped she'd be mollified when he told her he was "on the case."

"Big Sam's fish market, here I come."

THREE

"Six dollars a pound, Sam? Robbery." Lainey looked at the selection of orange roughy again. Maybe she'd go with the flounder. Aunt Minnie wouldn't be thrilled.

"Five-ninety-nine," Sam corrected, then raised his hands at her arched brow. "But for you I can maybe make a special. Five-fifty."

Lainey held his open gaze for several seconds, knowing Sam expected no less. Like her, he was a transplant from Philly. When Sam had heard from Minerva that her niece hailed from his hometown, he'd developed a special fondness for Lainey. Of course, Sam showed his fondness in his own unique way.

"Still robbery, Sam. I could go down to Fred's on Fiftieth and—"

"That crook wouldn't know a shark steak from a salmon. You don't buy from him." He looked appropriately outraged, but Lainey didn't miss the gleam in his eye. He appreciated a good haggler. "You buy from me, or I'll tell your dear sweet aunt Minerva that her niece is harassing the café's best supplier."

Lainey folded her arms, thoroughly enjoying herself. "Who do you think sent me here?"

Sam chuckled. "You learned from the best too. Don't you ever forget it."

"Think she'd let me?" Lainey countered with a wry grin. "Now, about these underfed roughy you're trying to pawn off on me."

Eyes twinkling, he wiped his hands on his ever-present apron. "Five dollars even. But you take some flounder too. Tell your aunt they'll be great stuffed with shrimp."

"Done. I'll need four pounds of tiger shrimp. And don't try to sneak any of those small ones in there."

Shaking his head, Sam sighed as if mightily offended and turned toward the back room. "Be right back. Stay out of trouble for a minute."

Lainey rolled her eyes, smiling at his retreating form. Her parents had passed away while she was in her midtwenties, leaving Conrad and his mother as her only connection to her hometown. While Lainey didn't miss the people she'd left behind in Philly, she did miss the city itself. The smells, the sounds, its color and vibrancy. Sam had given some of that back to her. For that alone she'd have paid the five-ninety-nine. Of course, she'd die before telling him that.

The sound of slow handclaps directly behind her caused her to turn around. "Tucker."

He acknowledged her less-than-enthusiastic greeting with a quick nod. "Madelaine. The way you handled old Sam there, I'd swear you were Lillian's niece, not Minerva's."

"Lainey," she corrected automatically, not entirely surprised to see him. She'd had a strange feeling that he'd pop up at some point. Still, she was surprised she hadn't felt his presence behind her. It was the intensity of that very thing that had kept her looking over her shoulder all afternoon.

She deliberately pushed aside any and all memories of her intoxicating morning spent at the all-too-willing mercy of those talented hands. Goose bumps of remembered pleasure raced over her skin, anyway. She hoped he didn't notice. In a life marked by impulsive choices, Tucker Morgan was another bad decision waiting to be made. But not this time. Not by her.

She gave him what she hoped was a confident but not-too-friendly smile. "So what brings you to Sam's?"

"You."

She'd never heard so much intensity packed into one tiny little word. Her heart skipped a beat without permission. She should have expected the direct approach from him, but she silently acknowledged that no amount of advance preparation would have squelched her instant reaction. Conrad and Charlie had been proof enough that her impulses should be curbed, not encouraged. After Charlie, she'd vowed to work on thinking things through calmly and rationally instead of jumping right in. She'd slipped a bit this morning, but she was firmly back on the wagon now.

She curved her mouth into a dry smile. "Well, that's direct. Or didn't you have a convenient excuse?"

"Do I need one?" he countered, his own smile making it clear that he was enjoying himself immensely.

So was she. She felt her wagon start to rock a little. *Hurry up, Sam,* she silently implored, *I'm treading dangerous waters out here.* "I suppose not. As they say"—she gestured blithely to the interior of Sam's shop—"it's a free market."

His gaze was unwavering. "But you'd feel better if I made one up, wouldn't you?"

Beating Tucker at his own game was a foolhardy strategy at best.

"Probably," she said. "I suppose it would be an easier world if people were more direct about what they wanted. In my experience, it's usually quite the opposite, and though I am trying to improve, I'm still occasionally guilty of being one of them. But in the spirit of self-improvement, I'll make another stab at it right now. Tell me, Mr. Morgan, exactly what is it you want of me?"

He clapped his hands slowly. "Not a bad start. And you sounded oh-so-proper too. Nicely done."

Lainey found herself trapped by his gaze. His eyes were making it crystal clear that he hadn't forgotten one single second of their less-than-proper encounter that morning. But the man was a professional, she argued. Certainly her very average body and less than sparkling wit hadn't driven him to the boundaries of his control . . . as his hands had driven her?

She snapped her gaze away from his and turned around, suddenly fascinated by the display of tiger shrimp and not feeling the least twinge of guilt over the pretense. Being straightforward wasn't all it was cracked up to be. At least not where Tucker Morgan was concerned.

She glanced over her shoulder. "My mother-in-law would be thrilled to hear that anyone thought me proper. Despite exhaustive attempts to mold me, she swore that 'proper' was an adjective that would never be used in conjunction with Madelaine Marie Maitland."

Instead of the expected chuckle, his gaze sharpened

further. She swore that she could feel the heightened alertness in the air. Fish fumes, she told herself. Toxic fish fumes.

"I thought you said you weren't married."

"I'm not," she said, returning her attention to the black-and-gray-striped shellfish. "Divorced. I'm plain old Lainey Cooper again."

"There is nothing remotely plain about you. And you're molded just fine, if you ask me. Your former mother-in-law must not be too fine a judge of character."

A vision of the horrified expression that would have marred Agatha Maitland's scrupulously maintained and dignified manner upon hearing that personal indictment had Lainey stifling a laugh. Dismissing the compliment, but intrigued by the absolute certainty of his pronouncement, she abandoned her fascination with the shrimp. She straightened and turned around. "And I suppose you are?"

"It was more or less my business."

"Knowing a person's character determines how you go about massaging them, Mr. Morgan?"

"Tucker. And I wasn't talking about massages. I told you, you were my first client. Ever. It's a, uh, recent career move for me."

"That's right, you're here to help out Lillian." Swapping verbal volleys with Tucker could be as much fun as it was with Sam, providing she didn't take him too seriously. Although the adrenaline pumping through her veins at the moment felt entirely different from the rush she'd gotten over getting a dollar off a pound of orange roughy. "So what career did you move from that required you to make snap judgments on people's characters?"

His grin was all together too disarming. She felt her

wagon pick up speed, and she struggled to keep a firm hold on her seat. Although, her little voice argued, if he was only there temporarily, what harm could there be in a little simple flirtation?

Simple? She smothered a self-deprecating chuckle. Hadn't she just finished deciding there was nothing simple about flirting or anything else when it came to Tucker Morgan? Her gaze flitted to the stuffed shark mounted on the far wall. A very visual, not to mention timely, reminder of why she shouldn't play with the big fish.

"I guess you could say I was a professional bodyguard," he answered.

Bodyguard? Oh, but that's too good, her hormones chimed in. Her mind betrayed her, too, providing full color Kevin Costner–Whitney Houston flashbacks as her wagon careened wildly out of control. She crossed her arms over her suddenly exquisitely sensitive and likely very noticeable nipples.

"Bodyguard?" She made a discreet attempt to clear the rasp from her throat. "You protected people?" It proved impossible not to look over the body that he'd used to protect them with. His blue eyes were twinkling when hers found their way back to his face. There was no way to hide the blush she felt creeping up her neck.

"Yep," he said. "They paid me and everything."

"What made you quit? I mean, why did you go from protecting bodies to massaging them?"

It might have been her imagination, but his eyes seemed to lose a bit of their shine, and his smile suddenly looked more forced than natural.

"I'm sorry," she said quickly. "That's none of my business."

He shrugged, the flicker of hesitation gone. "Hey,

you wanted to know, you asked. You were being direct, right?"

"It's being direct without being rude that sometimes trips me up."

"Now we're back to what's proper. Perhaps that was why your ex-mother-in-law had so much trouble passing on the concept."

"Oh, she had rude down to a science. But she managed to convey it ever-so-properly, so there were few who would dare to call her on it."

"I take it you were numbered among that few."

She gave a short laugh. "That was me. One of the few, the proud, the disowned."

"You seem to be doing all right without the formidable Maitlands."

"That's a matter of opinion," she said darkly, then grinned. "I, however, happen to agree with you. I'll ignore the fact that you don't know me very well."

"Which brings us to your earlier question. Or should we say, direct request?"

Her eyebrows furrowed. "Which was?"

"You asked me why I was here. I'm here because I don't know you very well and I'd like to remedy that situation." He raised his hand to stall her response. "I know you're busy, that's why I came to Sam's."

"To get to know me while I buy fish?" She paused as another thought struck her. "And how did you know I'd be at Sam's, anyway?"

Good question, Tucker. He could hardly tell her the truth. Not at this point, anyway. Yet their discussion about the virtues of being direct had him shifting uncomfortably at the idea of telling her an out-and-out lie. "I mentioned to Lillian that I was going to stop by Minerva's for lunch, and in the course of our conversation she mentioned something about you buying fish at Sam's today." Not exactly the truth, but bottom line, Lillian was his source of information about Sam's, so he didn't feel too much like pond scum.

"So you came down here to . . . what?"

To question you on your relationship with a man who appears to be involved in something shady with your aunt. That might be the direct response, but he was pretty certain it would also not get him the information he needed. And in the spirit of being straightforward, at least with himself, it wasn't the only reason he'd followed her down there. He liked plain old Lainey Cooper. A lot.

"To spend a little free time with a woman who intrigues me. How's that for direct and forthright?" He added, "No pressure, Lainey. I mean, we're at a fish market."

"But isn't there some code or something about professional masseurs and their clients?"

"You mean getting to know a client away from work?" He was beginning to wish he'd never agreed to help Lillian, much less in the role of masseur. It was only his first day, and already he was getting too tangled up in the deception. Of course, he wouldn't have met Lainey—at least not in such an interesting manner.

She nodded.

He had no idea what the code of ethics was. "Were you planning on scheduling regular appointments with me?"

He tried not to smile as her skin flushed a deep, delightful shade of red. He was finding himself very drawn to the sexy way she shifted back and forth, at one point gutsy then the next modest. He never knew how she'd react, which was half the fun of provoking her. On second thought, he might owe Lillian a thank-you. He suspected that if he'd met Lainey Cooper through any of the normal, more acceptable social channels, he wouldn't have seen these multifaceted elements of her personality. At least not quickly enough to become so intrigued.

"No, I hadn't really planned to—" At his feigned hurt expression she hastened to add, "Not that it wouldn't be wonderful. I mean, I told you how much I enjoyed it." If it was possible, her neck grew even splotchier. She groaned, then looked away. He thought he heard her mutter something about "understatement" as she turned her back to him.

He closed the distance between them and laid a hand on her shoulder, making her jump slightly. She stilled but didn't turn around.

He hadn't realized how badly he needed to touch her again. Even a light touch on her shoulder set off rockets of awareness in him. "Lainey," he said gently. "I didn't mean to embarrass you. If it would make you feel better, I could explain in great detail exactly how I felt about our morning session." Or, for that matter, how he was feeling right now, he added silently.

She whirled around, having to back up a step when she collided with his chest. He caught a fleeting glimpse of what that brief contact did to the front of her T-shirt and worked hard at keeping his eyes trained directly on hers.

"No, really, that isn't necessary." She took a breath and stepped back, but came up short against the display case. "What I mean is, even if I don't ever see you again professionally, I don't think it's . . . appropriate for me to . . . for us to . . ."

"You wouldn't feel comfortable seeing me because of how we met, is that it?"

She sighed in relief. "That's exactly it." She laughed self-consciously, but he could see her relaxing. "I'm glad you understand."

"Can I ask you one thing?"

Her relaxed expression tightened a bit, but even as it did, he saw her eyes take on that hint of determination that clued him in to another facet of her character. He watched in fascination as she straightened her shoulders and her grin grew more confident. The bold Lainey was back.

"Only if you take about three steps back." She fanned a hand in front of her chest. "Don't take this the wrong way, but you are a bit, well, intense."

He laughed. "No one has ever mentioned my intensity to me before."

"Well, I'm sure they thought it. Take it from me, you've got it nailed. I imagine it served you well in your former career. You're going to be very successful in your new line of work too. But can I make a suggestion?"

You can make anything you want, he wanted to say. "Shoot."

"After you leave Lillian's, you might want to think about getting a position where the clientele is a bit younger. Not that the older ladies won't love you, but their hearts aren't what they used to be, you know?" She folded her arms, apparently satisfied that she'd protected both herself and senior women everywhere from his potentially lethal clutches. "Now what was it you wanted to ask me?"

What are you doing for, oh, say, the next forty or fifty years? was the response that leaped immediately to his mind. It jolted him right out of his love-struck, hormone-driven stupor.

Whoa. Slow way down here, Morgan. Changing your life in order to open up your options is one thing, but you don't want to go falling in love with the first person under seventy-five you lay your eyes on.

She smiled at him.

Do you?

No, you don't, he answered emphatically. He was there to help Lillian solve a mystery, not find a wife. Hell, he didn't even know where he was going to live two weeks from now. He had plenty of whats and wheres to sort out in his life before he started thinking about the who he might share it with.

He quickly pulled himself together. "Can you get me a good deal on some of those shrimp?"

Her mouth dropped open, but she quickly snapped it shut. "Shrimp?"

Tucker stepped past her and scanned the array of shellfish with the interest of a man who hadn't eaten in a month. She turned and looked with him, as if by doing so she'd figure out what the sudden fascination was.

"I missed lunch," he explained, not caring how lame he sounded. So he'd lost his mind there for a few hours, it wasn't the end of the world. "These look good. I heard you haggling with Sam and figured you might be able to get him to cut me a deal."

A loud thump brought both their heads up. White-wrapped packages covered one end of the counter. Sam stood behind the counter, eyeing them both with unconcealed interest.

"A deal on what?" Sam said, eyes gleaming. He turned to Lainey. "And you stay out of this."

Tucker left Sam's fish market ten minutes later with a very good price on a pound of medium tiger shrimp. He'd left behind a woman who, despite his better judgment, fascinated the hell out of him, and a very nosy shopkeeper who he'd bet was popular in a town full of ladies whose favorite pastime was probably gossip. He sighed. Hell, Sam would probably have them married with three kids by sundown.

Tucker paused at the curb. He was certain that that thought should bother him more than it did. He had also left without getting a shred of information about Lillian's mystery. And his only contact? The woman he'd just forced himself to walk away from without a backward glance.

That capped it. He was definitely going to strangle Lillian. An easy job, she'd said. A couple of weeks, she'd said. It'll be like a vacation, she'd said. His first day as a detective, and he was already hopelessly entangled. For a man who'd just simplified his life, this didn't bode well.

"At least you got a good deal on lunch," he muttered as he crossed the street to his rental car. A raw lunch, he thought as he tossed the bag onto the passenger seat. Maybe he could get the kitchen at the hotel to steam them for him. Right after his chat with Aunt Lillian.

Lainey almost tripped over Ida's cane going through the back door of the café. The mesh bag of navel oranges wobbled precariously on top of the heavy cardboard box filled with dry ice and seafood that Sam had packed for her. She struggled to get through the door, barely making it to the counter.

"Well, it's about time," Irma said from her perch on the stool by the swinging doors that led to the front of the café.

"Now, Irma," Ida said, her voice pinpointing her whereabouts on the metal chair by the back door.

With a grunt, Lainey heaved the box onto the counter, then wiped her hair from her forehead as she turned around to face the twins. "Ladies," she greeted them. "Mr. Max," she added, nodding to the small dog peeking from Irma's bag in a play for time. "Why aren't you up front enjoying your coffee and pie?" As if she didn't know. She'd stalled as long as she could, wasting time she didn't have in the hopes that they'd have given up by now. She should have known better. Wasn't dealing with Tucker—twice—enough of a trial for one day?

She faced their determined expressions. Apparently not.

"Any more pie, and I'll have to go back to Bunny Macafee's Senior Stomp aerobics class," Irma groused. "Lord, I hate that woman. And someone ought to tell her it's downright disgusting to see someone her age strapped into spandex."

"I believe you did," Ida offered. "Right before she kicked you out of the class for insubordination."

Irma harrumphed. "Should have been a drill sergeant. I'm amazed someone hasn't dropped dead in there from a heart attack."

"Her classes aren't that strenuous," Ida said.

"I was talking about saccharine overload." She turned to Lainey, who was struggling not to laugh. "Have you heard the woman? Sounds like the sugarplum fairy on helium."

Lainey had met Bunny. She was a casual friend of Minerva's and a client of Lillian's who occasionally dropped in at the café. And in this case Lainey agreed with Irma. The woman was a high-strung, Minnie Mouse sound-alike, a born-again fitness nut who never missed an opportunity to lecture Lainey on the evils of fat grams. She all but claimed Minerva was killing the population of Sunset Shores by not modifying her menu. Aunt Minerva had long since tuned her out, but Lainey hadn't been in town a month when Bunny had swooped down on her like a vulture on fresh roadkill. Bless Minerva's kind heart, but Lainey didn't know how she put up with the woman.

"I've heard her," Lainey told Irma. "And I'm in complete agreement with you. Although I have to give her one thing."

"What?" the twins asked simultaneously.

"She looks better in a leotard than I do."

Irma snorted. "That's only because she dragged the name of Lillian's plastic surgeon out of her. I'm surprised he hasn't retired on her bills alone."

"Now, Irma, really," chided Ida.

"Well, at least Lillian admits that's why her fanny doesn't hang to her knees."

"I thought she got herself a personal trainer? That wrestler person, Sven the Avenger or something."

"Sven the Destroyer," Irma corrected, making Lainey stifle a snort despite her irritation. "And even he can only halt the vagaries of time for so long, Ida."

"Ladies," Lainey interjected, then immediately regretted it when they both turned their attention back to her.

"And speaking of Lillian," Irma said, drilling her with a sharp gaze. "How did your appointment go?"

Lainey folded her arms and leaned back against the counter. "First, tell me exactly why you sent me there without mentioning that the new Helga was a man."

To her credit Irma didn't even blink. "Because someone had to give him a test drive, and we figured you'd think we were meddling old women if we told you Lillian's masseuse was a man."

She didn't want to hurt their feelings. Despite Irma's brusque attitude, she knew Irma really cared about her. "I thought we all agreed after Charlie that you two wouldn't interfere in my love life again."

"Did I say anything about your love life?" Irma retorted. "I just wanted to know if he was any good." She leaned closer, her faded gray eyes sparkling. "So was he?"

Ida leaned forward. "Did he ask you out, dear?"

"He's unmarried," Irma added.

Ida nodded, her eyes twinkling too. "And a real hunk."

Lainey sighed. The gentle route was obviously not working. "I don't care if he's an unmarried hunk. I'm not interested in dating right now."

"Where is he taking you?" Ida scooted her chair forward. Even Mr. Max was sitting up with his ears perked at full attention.

"Who said he asked me out? I didn't—"

"For heaven's sake, I hope you didn't say yes right away," Irma said flatly. "It's not as if you have any competition around here. Don't be too eager, or he'll think you're easy."

"Irma!" Ida pressed her hand to her chest.

Irma sniffed. "Just looking out for our Madelaine, Ida. If she'd have been more careful with Charlie, she'd have probably—"

"Ended up exactly how I did," Lainey said. "And I only went out with him on your sterling recommendations and so your feelings wouldn't be hurt."

Both of their expressions immediately fell, leaving Lainey feeling as if she'd just kicked Mr. Max.

She sighed. "Listen, I appreciate that you care about me, I really do. But—"

"Don't let one bad apple sour you on the rest of the bunch," Ida said, jumping right back into it.

"Two bad apples," Irma said. "Remember her louse of a husband. And who knows how many before that."

"Irma, for heaven's sake, don't remind the dear girl of her failures."

"*My* failures?" Lainey said. She stopped abruptly and took a slow, deep breath. She should have known better than to fall for their pouts. After eighty years of practice, the sisters knew all the tricks and weren't the least bit afraid to use as many of them as they deemed necessary. Once decided on a course of action, nothing short of death would deviate them from their path. And she was almost convinced the sisters were immortal.

She had to find some way to end this right now. She'd made many bad choices in her life, number one on the list being her ex-husband, Conrad. She'd married him for all the wrong reasons, and in the end her impulsive choice had hurt them both. It had taken a lot of teeth gnashing for her to include her ex-mother-in-law in the category of innocent bystander, but two years and a thousand miles had made it a bit easier to be gracious. When she'd decided to stay in Florida, Lainey had also decided it was time to grow up and set some serious goals and guidelines for her life.

Then Charlie had come along, another prime example of Lainey making bad choices for the wrong reasons. But it had been a worthy lesson.

She took a breath and faced the sisters. "I appreciate your wanting to see me happy, really I do," she said earnestly. "But trust me, right now I'm happiest just being on my own. I highly recommend Tucker for his masseur skills, but as for anything else, I'm not interested. I'm serious about this and would appreciate it if you two would help me out. Okay?"

They both nodded, then made their good-byes, but Lainey didn't believe for a second that her little speech had convinced them to end their interference. But it didn't really matter, because her little speech had convinced her. Tucker had been a fun, harmless diversion. She'd consider her appointment that morning her last impulsive fling. But that was the beginning and the end of it. She was even proud of herself for recognizing it as such and not allowing his charm to flatter her into beginning any sort of relationship. She didn't need diversions in her life right now, particularly charming male ones, no matter how temporary.

Pleased with herself, she turned back to her purchases and began unpacking the seafood. Yes, she did have more important things to concentrate on than ex-bodyguard masseurs with heart-attack hands and knee-melting smiles.

Something was up with Minerva. A frown pulled at her mouth and concern wrinkled her forehead. Lainey didn't know exactly what and Minnie wasn't talking about it, at least not to her. She admitted that her aunt's silence hurt a bit, but it worried her more. Especially when she'd spied Damian Winters in town. Her conversation with him had been equally unrevealing.

She sighed a bit as she snugged memories of Tucker away in a back corner of her mind—for a final impulsive fling, he'd certainly been a worthy choice, one she'd enjoy recalling from time to time—but now she had to focus on life's important matters. Charming men weren't on that list, but her aunt Minerva topped it. She was all the family Lainey had left. One way or another, she had to find out exactly what her aunt was up to.

FOUR

Tucker reluctantly pushed through the door of the café. His talk with Lillian the previous afternoon hadn't gone exactly as planned. But then, when it came to Aunt Lillian, things rarely did.

He breathed a small sigh of relief when he spied an older woman, presumably Minerva, behind the counter. Maybe the gods would smile on him and Lainey would be off catering something.

Lillian had ignored his arguments for discontinuing his new occupation and, with her typical buzzard-eye style, zeroed in on his comments about Lainey. She was convinced that Lainey was his key to solving the mystery, and nothing he had said could deter her. He'd also perceived a healthy dose of matchmaking fervor underscoring her plans, which he hadn't even attempted to fight. It would only have made her more determined. A frightening thought. As it was, he considered himself lucky that he'd gotten out of there by agreeing to drop by the café for lunch and a hoped-for chat with Lainey over coffee.

Tucker wasn't sure what *he* hoped for, but a quick exit from Florida was looking really good at this point.

"Well, hello," Minerva greeted him warmly. She was short and pleasantly soft in a way that spoke well of her cooking skills. Her dark hair, only mildly scattered with gray, was pulled back into a voluminous bun, and she wore a plain blue dress with a white apron tied over it. She welcomed him with a smile as she finished arranging slices of cake on an old-fashioned pedestal tray. There was a brush of flour on her cheek and a smear of what looked like chocolate frosting on the bib of her apron.

A far cry from Aunt Lillian, Tucker thought. Minerva looked like the quintessential grandmother. The kind of woman who probably fed strays. The kind of woman who'd likely believe even a half-decently told sad-luck story. The kind of woman who could get suckered into a scam because she was too kindhearted to see lies instead of truth.

He hadn't really known what to expect. Lillian's stories over the past few years hadn't left a permanent memory in his mental file. He realized now, that since Minerva was Lillian's closest friend, he'd been expecting someone more like . . . well, like Aunt Lillian. One look told him this was a true case of opposites attracting. It didn't take any detective work to see why Lillian was so concerned. Minerva was a senior sucker waiting to be duped.

Tucker didn't know whether to groan at the additional helping of guilt or give Minerva a comforting hug and tell her he'd take care of everything. The urge to do both was equally strong. He settled for finding a spot at the counter and asking for coffee.

"Black?" she asked kindly. "Or do you like it sweet?"

Her eyes were brown, he noticed, unlike her niece's.

He recalled with disturbing clarity green eyes with flecks of gold. Cat eyes. "Black is fine," he said, blinking away thoughts of Lainey.

Minerva studied him for a second longer, but her twinkling eyes didn't reveal anything other than warm hospitality.

And what else would they show? he asked himself disgustedly. That she can see one thought of her niece had you almost squirming on your stool? He glanced down a bit too quickly as she slid the heavy, white ceramic mug in front of him. No use taking chances. One interfering busybody was enough. Minerva might look like a kindhearted granny, but Tucker had no doubt there was more than one matchmaking bone in her body. She had an unmarried niece. Meddling came with the territory.

"You must be Tucker," she said as she wiped down the counter. "I was wondering if you would pay us a visit."

Warily, he glanced up at her, but her expression was completely guileless. "I only started working for her yesterday." He should have waited until the café was busier. He was its only customer now. He swore his stool grew increasingly warmer under Minerva's steady regard.

"And I suspect you're already busy," she said easily. "At least if Lainey is to be believed. She says you'll make the ladies around here forget all about Helga."

Lainey had talked to her about him? With a determined mental shove, he pushed aside any questions he might have been tempted to ask. "I'm flattered to hear that." He smiled. A sip of coffee warmed him further. He could handle this.

Minerva paused in front of him. "You'll pardon me for saying this, but if you're half as good with your hands as you are to look at, I imagine you'll be booked up solid by the end of the week."

Tucker barely kept from choking on his coffee. He now knew exactly why Minerva and Lillian were close friends. "I'm, uh . . ." He paused to clear his throat. Her eyes sparkled so innocently, but Tucker was beginning to reevaluate who the gullible one was there. He'd spent years making sure the wrong people didn't get to those he was in charge of protecting, honing his observational and character-judgment skills to a keen edge. He rarely misjudged someone. In this instance his blind spot was probably caused by wishful thinking. "I'm only helping Lillian out temporarily."

"So I hear." She patted his hand. "But I give even odds that if you start booking them in, Lillian will find a way to keep you."

"At least you gave me a fighting chance," he said dryly.

She topped off his coffee. "Oh, I imagine if anyone could give Lillian a good run, it would be you."

Tucker took another sip as he let that comment sink in. Her tone had been warmly sincere. So what was she implying? He already realized that Minerva was far sharper than her homemade-pie personality let on, but did she know who he really was?

"I have no idea what Lainey said about me that would give you that idea." He gave her his best charming grin. "But I'll take it as a vote of confidence."

She smiled back, her eyes as guilelessly merry as ever. Tucker braced himself.

"Not to sound critical, but Lainey hasn't always been the best judge of character when it comes to men. After the Charlie fiasco, she decided—wisely, if you ask me—to step back and examine her mistakes and figure out what keeps getting her in trouble. I told her she needs to spend more time thinking things through. Jackrabbits have more patience than our Lainey. Of course, she managed to resist you—though heaven knows why she picked now to put my advice to the test." She gave him a once-over that made him squirm on his stool, then sighed and shook her head. "I love her dearly, but the girl has no sense of timing."

Tucker wasn't completely sure, but he thought he'd just been flattered. Not that it mattered. He was there to get Minerva out of whatever trouble she'd gotten into, not to impress her *or* her niece on his suitability as a potential mate.

Minerva brushed a quick hand over her hair, smoothing back a few loose wisps from her plump cheeks. "I said what I did because Lillian has faith in you, or she wouldn't have hired you. That makes points with me. She doesn't hire anyone who can't give as good as they get. She says she's too old to modify her temperament." Minerva's laugh was as delightfully rich and full-bodied as the woman herself. "I think she simply likes to keep her scissors sharp, if you know what I mean."

Tucker found himself laughing with her. He understood Lillian's affection for the woman. It was impossible not to like Minerva Cooper.

A buzzer went off somewhere back in the kitchen. After topping off his coffee, Minerva placed the pot on the warmer and bustled off to the back with the empty tray on which she'd brought the cake out, leaving Tucker to his coffee and contemplation. Apparently round one was over.

His mind returned unerringly to her comments about

Lainey. Hasty decisions? Impatient? And who was Charlie and why was he a fiasco? Tucker thought her ex-husband's name was Conrad.

All questions he had no business thinking about, he reminded himself. He had come in there only to find out who the guy was Lainey'd been seen talking to at Sam's last week. Another bad judgment call on her part? If this guy was bad news, maybe Lillian's ladies were doing what came naturally: meddling. Tucker could easily see them banding together to warn the guy off. The secrecy also made sense if they didn't want Lainey to know about their interference—a highly probably scenario. But why hadn't Minerva enlisted Lillian's help in the scheme? Or maybe she thought the matter resolved and unimportant.

The mental swirl of questions scattered as the doors to the back swung forward. Minerva pushed into the room holding a steaming pan of muffins. Blueberry, he thought, unable to keep from inhaling the sweet scent. His stomach growled.

She stopped in front of him, dropping a hot pad onto the counter, then placing the tray on it. "So," she said without preamble, "exactly how do you know Lillian? She's been remarkably closemouthed about you."

A bell rang inside his head. Round two. Minerva didn't need a personal trainer. She packed a pretty good punch with oven mitts and an apron.

"I'm an old acquaintance," he said as smoothly as possible.

"Muffin? Blueberry, homemade," she added with a grandmotherly smile. But he knew better now. This was bribery, pure and simple.

The sweet-smelling steam wafted beneath his nose. "Sure," he said, telling himself it was merely a play for time. She arranged an oversized muffin on a plate with a small side cup filled with creamy butter and set it in front of him. He made a mental note to call the hotel and set up another tennis match for him against one of the staff pros. Or better yet, he'd run all the way back to Seattle.

"I figured she must have known you from before she moved to Sunset Shores and opened A Cut Above. Did you work for her at her salon in Winter Haven?"

Bending the truth was one thing, outright lying was another. "No," he said nicely but firmly. "It was a nice place, though. Did you know her then?" That's the ticket, turn the tables. Weren't detectives supposed to be the ones asking the questions, anyway?

"Heavens, no," she said, busily arranging the muffins on another tray. He knew better than to think that the task distracted her one iota from the conversation at hand.

"She seems very happy here," he went on. "I know she enjoys your friendship. She's spoken very highly of you." Minerva placed the last muffin, and he hurried on to the next question. "How long have you owned the café?"

"Ten years. I came out here from Pensacola when my Mervin died." As if sensing his immediate thought, she laughed briefly and said, "Yes, Minerva and Mervin. We took quite a bit of ribbing. But, oh, what a match we made." Her laughter faded to a smile illuminated by what must have been wonderful memories, judging by the way her eyes misted slightly.

Tucker felt that empty place he'd discovered inside himself after Pete's death yawn a bit wider. What would it feel like to love someone so deeply that the slightest mention of them brought tears to a person's eyes even years after their death?

"I can't believe you've known Lillian so long and she's never mentioned you," she said, yanking him back to the present.

He was blessedly saved from further grilling when the bells on the door tinkled. Another customer. He silently prayed for an early-lunch horde. But a quick glance showed him that it was only one person. Another senior. A worried senior, judging by the way she rushed to the counter, her penciled brows furrowing deep lines in the heavily powdered space between them.

"Good morning, Betty Louise," Minerva greeted her.

Betty Louise didn't acknowledge the greeting. She leaned over the counter as far from where Tucker was sitting as possible and said in a hushed whisper that they could both plainly hear, "I must talk to you, Minerva. Right away."

"Certainly," she said calmly, as if overanxious customers were a normal occurrence. For all Tucker knew, maybe they were. She turned to him and said, "Help yourself to another muffin—"

"Really, Minerva, it can't wait." Betty Louise twisted the white gloves she held in her hands until Tucker half thought she might wrench them in two. The woman was really upset. "I tried to call Bernice, but she's at her sister's this weekend. It's urgent, I tell you. I just saw . . ." She shot a glance at Tucker and her frown deepened, then she cupped one hand at the corner of her mouth, blocking his unabashed view. "You-know-who. And he was talking to . . ." She glared at him again. "You-know-who."

Minerva merely smiled. "Now, now, don't go getting

all riled up, you'll have a spell." She turned quickly to Tucker and said, "I'll be back in a few minutes." She picked up her oven mitts and went to the end of the counter. She flipped the latch, allowing Betty Louise behind the counter, then patted her arm. "Have you taken your medication this morning, dear?" Tucker heard Minerva ask as they disappeared through the swinging doors.

Betty Louise. Bernice. The other two members of the group involved in this mystery. He sat there for a full minute, debating the wisdom of what his gut was telling him to do. And it was not to wolf down another blueberry muffin, though they were, hands down, the best he'd ever tasted.

He shot a quick glance over his shoulder, then slid off the stool and walked to the end of the short counter. He leaned over and flipped the latch. If caught, he could always say he was getting the coffeepot. He didn't think Minerva would mind the intrusion. He went for the pot, then hovered back near the swinging doors, straining to hear the hushed conversation taking place in the back room.

If he was lucky, he'd get the name of the guy without having to talk to Lainey at all. Then he could make some contacts and, he hoped, find out something about him that would answer Lillian's concerns, ending this stupid game once and for all. Then Tucker could get back to the matter at hand.

He conveniently refused to think about the fact that the matter at hand was figuring out exactly what the matter at hand should be. Mapping out a new life was not as smooth an operation as he'd anticipated. He knew he no longer wanted his old life, but he was no closer now than when he'd sold his business to figuring out exactly what it was he did want, much less how to go about getting it.

His mind made a straight line from that thought to Lainey Cooper. There was no denying that both his encounters with her had exhilarated him in a strange internal way he couldn't recall ever feeling before. She challenged him on a level he'd never approached before. "Repressed hormones," he murmured under his breath.

He shook his head—in disgust or denial, he couldn't say—and again resolutely shoved Lainey Cooper out of his mind. He also shoved aside the thought that in very little time she seemed to have carved out quite a big spot inside his brain. What little he had left, he thought, reviewing his current circumstances.

Sighing in resignation, he leaned a little closer to the swinging doors, figuring he had time to move to a safe, innocent-looking distance if he heard the ladies heading back.

"Moonlighting as a short-order cook?" came a dry voice from behind him.

Lainey. Tucker swung around, holding the pot away from his body as coffee sloshed over the rim. He swore as the hot liquid scalded his fingers, and he quickly moved to put the pot on the counter. "Do you have some paper towels back here for spills?" he asked in lieu of answering her. Maybe if he took long enough to clean up this mess, he'd think of some way to explain himself. He had no idea how long she'd been standing behind him, but it had probably been long enough to cancel out his coffee-refill excuse.

"Under the counter, on the shelf below the cake dome."

"Thanks." He'd been so wrapped up in his thoughts

about her, he hadn't heard the bells on the door. Getting caught red-handed—literally—did not speak well of his burgeoning career as a detective; a fact that, except for his affection and concern for Lillian, did not disturb him.

He mopped the floor until he could see his reflection in it and was still no closer to a believable explanation. So he'd wing it. It had been his brilliant strategy to date. He stood up and wasted another two seconds pitching the wad of wet paper towels into the trash.

"Is your hand okay?"

He turned to find Lainey seated on the stool he'd foolishly vacated earlier. He glanced down and stared absently at the angry red mark marring his thumb and the back of his hand. In his mind's eye all he saw was Lainey. In cuffed white shorts and a red-and-white-striped sleeveless blouse—one that she'd knotted at the waist so that she could torment him with the peekaboo skin above her navel—she easily replaced Barbara Eden at the top of his lifelong list of women whose belly buttons he'd kill to see.

Considering he'd already seen her in a good deal less, his response was surprising. Or should be. He was quickly realizing that where Lainey Cooper was concerned, life was one unexpected emotional twist after another.

"Just a minor burn," he said.

She slid off the stool and took his hand in hers. After a quick examination that left other body parts of his far more inflamed, she let him go. "I have just the thing for it."

"Really, that's not—" He stopped himself. She was giving him time he'd be wise to take. "Thanks, I'd appreciate it."

She opened the latch, then moved into the suddenly very narrow space behind the counter. He watched mutely as she reached for one of the small metal condiment containers lined up on the narrow preparation table that fronted the wall separating the café area from the kitchen. She drained the juice from it into a bowl and turned to him. "Here."

"I thought you meant aloe or a burn ointment."

"This is better."

He didn't have to sniff the contents, he'd seen what the container had held before she drained it. Skeptically, he eyed the light green liquid, then her. "Pickle juice?"

She smiled reassuringly. "Yes. Don't ask, just dunk your hand. Do it quickly, it works best if you do it right away."

"Whatever you say, Doc." He had to do it in stages, but the relief was instant. "Amazing. Thanks."

She shrugged and handed him a wet towel to wipe his hand. "The things you learn working in food preparation. Minerva is a gold mine of homeopathic remedies like these."

"Handy to have around." His mind wasn't on Aunt Minerva as he spoke.

She tidied up, then leaned against the counter. "So now that we've cleaned and tended, would you mind telling me what you were doing back here?"

Another bell went off. Round three. Looking into her no-longer-so-reassuring cat eyes, he thought maybe he'd rather go another round with Minerva after all. Hell, she could tag-team with Lillian and he'd still have better odds than the ones he was facing. "Topping off my coffee?" He had to at least give it a shot.

She didn't even bother to respond.

"I was worried about Minerva." *My, Tucker,* he

thought, *you're becoming a regular master at bending the truth*.

Lainey's eyes immediately clouded over with concern. "Did something happen? Is she okay?" She started to push past him, but he gently grabbed her arms, holding her still.

"She's fine," he said. "I didn't mean to alarm you. I'm sorry. She's in the back talking to Betty Louise Strickmeyer. Actually, it's Mrs. Strickmeyer who's upset."

He'd swiftly debated on whether to mention Betty Louise by name but then decided that watching Lainey's reaction might provide some insight into the situation. He had a pretty good idea that Lainey was one of Betty Louise's "you-know-whos."

He wasn't sure what he'd been hoping for, but it wasn't the unreassuring wariness that suddenly colored her expression. "Oh," she replied, her smile a bit too forced. "Betty Louise is a good friend of Minerva's. She's a dear, but she is a little high-strung. I'm sure Minerva will take care of whatever is bothering her. She's good with people that way." Lainey moved out of his grasp and turned back to the counter, busying herself by cleaning up the ring left by the coffeepot.

This was the Lainey he'd seen, albeit briefly, when they'd first met. Wary, uncertain, uncomfortable. Her change in character bothered him. He didn't like to think he made anyone uncomfortable. And he much preferred the Lainey who boldly challenged him, then forced him to deal with his unprecedented reactions. Mostly, however, it bothered him that for the first time he truly believed there might be some real foundation for Lillian's concerns. Just who was this other "you-know-who" and what had he gotten them all involved in?

"I'd say being a people person is a trait passed on from aunt to niece," Tucker said, proceeding on instinct.

She rinsed the towel in the stainless-steel sink next to the prep table. "What makes you say that? You hardly know me."

He noticed she still wasn't making eye contact. He turned and rested a hip on the table, only a foot away from her. "I know there are two older ladies out there who care enough about you to want to see you happy." That made her turn her head, but he raised a hand to still her defense. "And a blind person could see the affection in Sam's eyes when he's haggling with you."

She opened her mouth, then closed it again. After a short pause, she shrugged. "Okay, so I've made good friends here. I know it sounds odd to some, given the age difference, but I really enjoy the people of Sunset Shores. Most of them, anyway," she added with a pointed look and a dry smile.

He ignored the last part. "It shows," he said. "And I don't think it odd at all that you've formed attachments to the folks around here."

It suddenly occurred to him that perhaps her connection to the mystery man might in some way be related to her helping her aunt and their Sunset Shores friends. Maybe she'd been trying to do the same thing he was: find out who the guy was and make sure her friends and aunt weren't involved in anything that could hurt them. If the guy was into something "shady," as Lillian had put it, then Lainey would be wise to stay clear of him.

"A refreshing attitude," she said lightly. "And one that would have suited you well around here."

" 'Would have'?"

"If you were going to stay. You said you were only temporary."

That he had. He studied her openly. Just who are you, Lainey Cooper, and why can't I get you out of my head? he wanted to shout.

According to Minerva, she was someone who had no patience and who made hasty decisions. That may all be true, Tucker decided, but the Lainey Cooper in front of him also had inner strength, a keen intellect, and a big, kind heart. He thought the combination was rather delightful, foibles and all. Hasty decisions weren't all bad, not when the motivating factor was care and concern for others. And impatience could be a good foundation in motivating a person to get things done.

He avoided answering her comment about his temporary status and returned to his previous point. "I assume that there are others who do think it's odd?"

"Oh, I could give you a list, beginning with my former mother-in-law."

He was pleased to see that her expression remained open. He didn't want to shutter the life out of those wonderful eyes by probing too far, too soon. "I thought we already determined that your ex-mother-in-law was a poor judge of character."

"Boy, I could have used a guy like you back in Philly." Her eyes lit up with humor and something else. Something . . . wistful. Something . . . needy.

Something inside Tucker shifted, making his heart suddenly feel warmer, heavier, fuller. He realized he'd like nothing better than to come to her rescue. The idea of being needed by Lainey Cooper was a heady thing. He'd spent a good chunk of his life being a protector, but it had been pride and integrity in a job well done that had driven him to excel. This feeling, this urge she created inside him . . . it was baser, more primal. Personal. Possessive. Necessary in a way that had nothing whatsoever to do with job performance.

"Anytime, anywhere," he heard himself say, the words quiet yet unshakable. He was deeply gratified by the way her pupils shot wide and color rose to her cheeks.

"Beware of offers made in haste," she warned, but her wry tone was undercut with a huskiness that sizzled a path straight to his heart. Something of his feelings must have shown in his expression, because the humor faded from her eyes, leaving only wariness and maybe a hint of wistful need.

"I won't ever regret this one," he said softly.

She started to turn away, but something in her eyes, some flicker of vulnerability that pained him even more for being the cause of it, had him reaching out and touching her chin. He gently turned her face back to his, waiting for her to raise her gaze to his. Patience. *Yes*, he thought as he willingly lost himself in her green-gold eyes, *I have all the time in the world for you, Madelaine Cooper.*

"I didn't mean to make you uncomfortable," he said softly. "And it wasn't a line. I know we just met, but I meant what I said, Lainey." His gaze dropped to her lips and it was all he could do not to lower his mouth and let his kiss explain what he could not. He dragged his gaze back to hers. "If there is anything I can ever do, all you have to do is ask."

She searched his eyes. He didn't blame her for being wary, for looking for reassurance. Her lips parted, but she said nothing. Tucker drew closer, moved his head a fraction of an inch closer, then stopped. *Don't push*, he schooled himself. *Don't rush*. Hasty decisions. Impatience. Bad judgments. Not this time, he vowed, not with him.

"Lainey, I—"

The abrupt movement of the swinging doors had them all but leaping apart. Minerva bustled in, and if she was surprised to see the two of them behind the counter, she didn't show it.

On closer inspection, he noticed her eyes were on full twinkle. Tucker's eyes narrowed in suspicion. Just who had been eavesdropping on whom?

"I thought I heard you out here," she said to Lainey. "Betty Louise is having another one of her spells."

"I'm sure a slice of your yogurt chiffon pie put her to rights," Lainey said with what looked to Tucker like a relieved smile. She was relieved he hadn't kissed her?

And, oh, he wanted to kiss Lainey Cooper. If he were completely honest, he'd admit that kissing was only the beginning of what he wanted to do for, to, and with Lainey Cooper.

"Well, I thank you both for holding down the fort out here for me," Minerva said as she moved the coffeepot back to the warmer and rinsed out the pickle-juice bowl in the sink. She dried her hands on a fresh towel as she turned to face them both. "Of course, I have no idea what you're doing in here on your day off," she said to Lainey, then turned her warmest, most grandmotherly smile on Tucker. He resisted the urge to stand straighter. "She's such a dear, but she has no idea how to relax." Lainey sputtered, but Minerva talked right over her. "According to Lillian, neither do you," she added, quelling Tucker's smug smile and earning him a smirk from Lainey. "So why don't you both do yourselves a favor and go out and enjoy the sunshine? You'll have plenty of time to stay indoors when you're old and wrinkled like me."

Before he could figure out how to stop her, Tucker found himself standing next to Lainey on the sidewalk in front of the café.

"We've been evicted," he said.

"I'd say more like hornswoggled." She glanced back at the door. "I adore my aunt, but sometimes she's a wee bit pushy."

"Lainey, a handcart is a wee bit pushy. Your aunt Minerva is a bulldozer. But you gotta give her points on style."

"You're too forgiving, believe me."

"She's forever in my favor on the merits of her blueberry muffins alone." He rubbed his stomach with remembered reverence.

Lainey gasped in mock horror. "She tortured you with muffins? My God, man, I can't blame you for caving." She clasped a hand to her chest and leaned closer. In a dramatic tone she whispered, "Did you tell all?"

Chuckling, he shook his head. "Saved by Betty Louise Strickmeyer."

"Well, it's nice to know the woman's spells are good for something."

She'd said it teasingly, but Tucker had heard the underlying irritation. His mind jumped back to the you-know-who situation. "Yeah, she seemed a bit wired when she rushed in. I guess every circle has to have their drama queen."

"Please, whatever you do, spare us all and don't ever let her hear you say that."

He crossed his heart. "You have my solemn vow."

She smiled and nodded, but the silence grew from a brief pause to an uncomfortable lag. "Well, enjoy the rest of your day. Hope your hand is okay."

Tucker didn't want her to go. His reasons had little to do with the mystery he was in charge of solving, but it was as good a reason as any to keep her around. Whatever had caused Betty Louise's "spell" apparently involved Lainey, which meant she was tied up in this somehow. He wasn't sure if he should explain everything to her yet, but until he was, the best plan would be to keep her with him. "You in a hurry to go somewhere?"

Her expression sobered, and she shifted from one foot to the other. "Well, there are some things I should be—"

"There's a park near here, isn't there?" he asked, not giving her time to come up with an excuse.

"There's one two blocks from here, by the water-front."

"Do you have time to show me?"

"It's straight ahead that way," she said, pointing down the street behind him.

He gave her his most winning smile. "I get lost easily."

She propped her hands on her hips, but a smile kicked around the corners of her mouth. "There's a big body of water at the end of the street. It's called the Gulf of Mexico. You can't miss it. The park is right in front of it. If your feet get wet, you've gone too far."

"I appreciate that, but I still need you to come with me."

"Why do you *need* me to go with you?"

An amazing list of reasons why he needed her by his side sprang easily to mind, but he offered the one that was most likely to get him what he wanted.

"How else are you going to find out what I was really doing behind Minerva's counter?"

FIVE

He had her there, Lainey thought, her curiosity piqued despite her internal alarm system, which was telling her to vacate the premises immediately before she did something rash and foolish instead of doing the sensible thing, which was finding out what had caused Betty Louise's spell.

Had Betty Louise seen her talking to Damian? she wondered with renewed frustration. He'd cleaned up nicely since their days in college together, but he was still a weasel under the expensive clothes and polished speech.

She'd had another heart-to-heart with her aunt the previous day, and Minerva had finally admitted that she had become an investor in a land deal she'd heard about while catering a luncheon at the hotel several weeks earlier. Bernice and Betty Louise had been with her and had also decided to get in on the deal. Minnie hadn't wanted to discuss it because the window of opportunity had been small, and the three had decided to keep it to themselves so that no one's feelings would get hurt over not being included.

She hadn't discussed it with Lainey, because, after the incident with Charlie, she hadn't wanted to worry her niece unnecessarily. Lainey'd tried to question her further about the specifics of the deal but had gotten nowhere. Minerva had reassured her that it was a sound deal that would make her more comfortable in her retirement and to not worry about it any longer.

But Lainey was worried. Then she'd spotted Damian in town again and warning bells had gone off in her head. Minerva hadn't mentioned his name in conjunction with the company she'd dealt with—something Lainey had planned to track down that afternoon—but when she'd tried to get some answers, he'd smoothly evaded her questions and more or less politely warned her to back off.

"Lainey?"

She snapped her attention back to Tucker. She really didn't have time for this right now. Still . . . what *had* he been doing behind the counter?

Almost kissing you, that's what. Her body grew warmer at the memory of the intent way he'd focused on her mouth and how she'd felt when he'd started to move closer, his intentions clear in his dark blue eyes. She swallowed a sigh. Of relief? It should be, she scolded herself. She had no business thinking about, much less participating in, a kiss or anything else with Tucker Morgan.

She'd sworn to start being more practical, less impulsive. Her reaction to Tucker was all the proof she needed that she wasn't even close to achieving her goal. Her aunt and her friends needed her, and she needed to be calm and levelheaded if she was going to help them. She couldn't seem to be either around this bodyguard-turned-masseur.

"If you really have things to do—"

She almost jumped when he touched her arm. "I . . ." I really have to go, she prompted herself to say, but what came out was "I guess a short break won't hurt."

Any remorse she felt over her continued failure to rehabilitate herself was extinguished by his brilliant smile. The man was certainly not difficult to look at.

Conrad hadn't been either, she reminded herself. Yeah, but Conrad, sweet, rich, and rebelling against his family's stuffy attitudes—which had been a large part of why she'd impulsively decided to elope with him after a one-month whirlwind romance—had turned out to be a spineless wimp who quickly reverted to his mother's domineering control. So what if he happened to clean up nicely? He'd had the carte blanche help of his mother's charge accounts, New York City's finest personal tailors, and the entire staff at Estée Lauder. Despite the fact that her romantic bubble had burst shortly after the honeymoon, Lainey had stuck it out for seven years. Yet all of those things combined hadn't been enough to transform her into the proper society matron that Conrad and his mother were determined the wife of Conrad Maitland III must be.

Whereas Tucker . . . He only demanded that she be herself. And there was nothing remotely wimpy about his spine or anything else. He'd look good in a burlap sack. Or out of one for that matter. She abruptly shut off that train of thought and turned around. "Well, what are we waiting for?" she said a bit more briskly than she'd intended. "The gulf beckons."

She felt Tucker's gaze drilling into her back, but she refused to look at him or stop. If she were smart, she'd start running and never look back. *No, if you were smart,* her inner voice countered, *you'd be in the café right now politely grilling Betty Louise over yogurt chiffon, then tracking down that weasel Damian and finding some way to convince him to put an end to this mess.*

Instead she faced at least an hour at the park with the man she'd sworn to herself, not once, but several times, that she should stop spending any time with. *Not doing so good on this impulse thing, are you, Lainey?*

"Are you coming," she called out, irritated with herself and Tucker, "or are you going to stand there all day staring at my backside?"

He caught up to her easily. "Not that watching your rear end isn't an entirely worthy pastime, but I'd prefer your charming company instead."

She made a harrumphing sound worthy of Irma's best and strode on. She could see the sparkle of water in the distance. Almost there. She'd use the walk to plan her strategy, point out one or two points of interest to Tucker, then bail out and go back to the café. There, she felt better already. Maybe she had grown. Maybe she could handle Tucker after all. This was actually a good way to prove how much she'd changed.

He kept up with her accelerated pace while managing to keep his own stride loose and easy. "Call me old-fashioned, but I sort of imagined a stroll to the park."

"That's what we're doing," she answered between breaths.

"No, this is definitely not strolling. This is more like stomping. Or striding with fierce determination." When she scowled at him and sped up, he reached for her arm and forced her to slow down. "You know, I think your aunt is right. You have no idea how to relax."

Lainey stopped abruptly. Tucker almost dragged her

another two feet before he managed to switch gears and stop too.

"I can relax just fine," she said, pulling her arm from his grasp. "I simply can't relax around you." She hadn't meant to say that last part out loud, and his intent expression told her it was a mistake she was about to pay for dearly.

Eyes bright with heightened awareness, he stepped closer. She made herself stay where she was. She could resist him and his charm. She would. Had to. In fact, this challenge would be her personal gauntlet, she decided. Madelaine Cooper was going to prove once and for all that she could control her impulses and let her head rule her heart. And her hormones.

"And why do you think that is?" he asked. "What am I doing to make you tense up? We're just walking. Or trying to." He took another step.

Lainey stood straighter and held her ground, feeling like a gunslinger at high noon who was facing down the last fast gun. "It probably has something to do with the fact that we met under very unusual circumstances and I am having a hard time adjusting to . . . to . . ." He stepped closer. She swallowed hard. Even gunslingers got ten paces.

"What is there to adjust to, Lainey? You put one foot in front of the other, and before you know it, you're walking."

His too-amused expression rankled. She raised her chin. "This isn't about walking. You'll have to forgive me, but I'm not used to being nearly naked with a man one day—professionally naked that is," she added hurriedly, when something that wasn't close to amusement sparked in his blue eyes, "then dealing with him on a social level the next."

Proud of herself, she mentally blew the smoke from her steaming pistol.

He stepped even closer, angling his body so that he was directly in front of her, blocking the sun, which cast his face in deep shadows. "Exactly how many days, then, do you need?" he asked in a slow drawl that would make any fast gun proud. "Between being naked with me—professionally naked, that is—and being social?"

It was possible, she thought shakily, that she'd reholstered her gun a bit too quickly. Or perhaps her aim had been off.

"Nearly naked. I was nearly naked," she corrected, the distinction minor but for some reason crucial. "And there aren't enough days to make it okay. I thought we had this all settled back at Sam's."

" 'All this' being?"

"You know." She waved her hand in a jerky motion in the tiny space between them. "*This*. Us."

"We're an 'us'?"

Humor flickered in his oh-so-charming baby blues, along with what, to anyone else, probably looked like desire. Hot, deep, not easily quenched desire. But she wasn't fooled, no, not her. He didn't really desire her. It was the game, the chase. He was toying with her, she told herself. Yes, that was certainly it. And he had to be stopped before he . . . before she . . . Well, he just had to stop, period.

"No, we're not an 'us,' " she countered. "That's the whole point here. I'm a client and you're a . . . a . . ."

"Masseur?"

"A service professional," she corrected hastily but

firmly, ignoring the instant visuals the mere word *masseur* brought to mind. "And service professionals shouldn't confuse a client with a potential date."

"There is only one thing I'm confused about."

The space between them was rapidly shrinking, figuratively and literally. Her shots had gone wide. "What?" she asked, feeling the figurative pistol slip from her grasp. Oh, how did she get herself into these things?

"Do you plan to book future appointments with me?" he asked.

She saw the trap immediately. Hah, she'd show him. "Yes," she said on impulse, "in fact, I do. I—I was just telling Aunt Minerva this morning how wonderful you— That is to say, how professional you were and how skilled your hands—" She stopped and drew a short breath. "I'm still technically a client," she finished, clinging to one last scrap of pride.

"Then, as your service professional, I recommend a nice stroll to the park. A perfect way to relax tense muscles."

She blew out the breath she'd been holding. She'd never had a chance. "Sure. Why not." She stepped around him, focused her attention on the water ahead, and determined not to stop until she was ankle deep in it. Just because she'd lost the showdown did not mean she'd failed her gauntlet test. She'd gotten him to admit that their relationship was strictly professional, which was, the way she saw it, a point scored for her. Feeling better, she smiled.

He caught her arm before she'd gone even a foot. "Stroll, Lainey. Like this." He slid his hand along her shoulders as smoothly as if he'd been doing it for years. She fit against his side just as easily. He reached behind him with his free hand and tugged at her elbow, which was wedged between them. "And like this," he said, sliding her arm around his waist.

"This doesn't seem very professional to me," she said, but didn't quite manage to pull her arm away.

He slanted a glance at her. "I'm teaching you how to relax. Professional to client."

She eyed him warily.

"Think of how pleased Minerva will be."

Oh, she'd be pleased, all right, Lainey thought crossly. Despite her aunt's outward approval of Lainey's decision to abstain from a social life until she'd established some new boundaries for herself, she knew that, in Minerva's old-fashioned heart, *her* goal—along with half the citizens of Sunset Shores, it seemed—was to see Lainey happily married. Of course, even Minerva would have to agree that Tucker Morgan wasn't suitable means for achieving either of those goals. Wouldn't she?

Lainey slanted a quick look at Tucker's face. His expression was as easy and open as he was. Friendly. Handsome. Funny. Honest. And, she recalled, her arm tingling along the smooth sway of his waist, he had a really nice butt. He was solid and warm and . . . reassuring. Minerva probably loved him. And the fact that he was a personal friend and protégé of Lillian's had probably sealed her fate.

"What was that sigh for?" he asked. "Is this really bothering you?" He stopped and turned her to face him, holding her shoulders in his big, very capable hands. His teasing manner was gone. In fact, he looked remarkably sincere. "Okay, no more word games and subtle evasions. I enjoy your company, Lainey. In fact, I went to the café in the hopes of seeing you."

"I thought we—"

"Shh. Let me finish. A professional-client only relationship is not what I want, but I learned as a child that I don't always get what I want. I can take it, Lainey." He flashed a quick grin. "Okay, so I might pout and whine a little, but all us guys are little boys at heart. You'll have to cut me a little slack on that."

"Little boys at heart." He'd hit her biggest problem square on the nail head. Teasing grins. Sheepish explanations. Adorable pouts. Wheedling requests. They never failed to tug at her heart. Conrad had mastered them all. Which was why it had taken her so long to figure out how little he truly cared for her. Charlie had been smoother in his delivery, but she'd still been suckered right in.

And where had it gotten her? In the end, divorced and alone. She didn't blame the men in her life. Okay, maybe she blamed Charlie a little. But Conrad hadn't really pretended to be something he wasn't. She had chosen to be with Conrad, thinking the glimmers of strength she'd seen in him during their courtship could be nurtured, that because he'd stood up to his family by marrying her, he'd stand by her always. She'd been wrong. Marrying her had been his one and only act of strength. He'd caved in immediately afterward and become his mother's mouthpiece on how *she* should be the one to change.

Tucker wasn't a spineless Conrad or a manipulating Charlie. No, he was even more dangerous. He had all the good traits she was attracted to and, as far as she'd seen so far, none of the bad. He had drive and determination and would do what he had to to get what he wanted. Right now that seemed to be her. The very idea made her pulse pound, but that wasn't where the danger lurked. He was a temporary man. And even temporary men could break your heart. She wasn't willing to repair hers again.

She removed his hands from her shoulders, stifling a small, unexpected sigh over the fact that she'd never feel them kneading her flesh again, smoothing oil into her skin, working the tension from her muscles. . . . You know, she thought, idly rubbing her thumbs into his palms, she didn't have to give him up completely. She could still see him professionally. She could . . . She blinked her eyes open and dropped his hands as if they'd burned her.

Taking a step back, she looked at him. "I appreciate your honesty, Tucker, really I do. And I'm flattered that you're interested in me. To be honest, I find you interesting too. But . . ." She raised a hand to hold off his response. "But I've made some unwise decisions in my relationships with men. Actually, they were downright lousy. I'm not suggesting you're a lousy choice, but you yourself said you were only here temporarily. I'm having a hard enough time figuring out what I want. I do know that I don't need even a temporary distraction right now. Professional or personal." She took a breath, then realized there was nothing else to say except maybe "I'm sorry."

Tucker stared at her. There was no denying she was dead serious. He was stunned by the crushing sense of disappointment he felt at the prospect of never seeing her again. He had no idea what he'd had in mind as to their future relationship, only that he'd wanted one. But she was right. More right than even she knew. He *was* only temporary. His whole life was temporary. At least until he decided what his new life was going to be. It certainly wasn't being a masseur for Lillian, nor was investigating the mystery man of Sunset Shores a lifetime occupation. Hell, he wasn't even planning on staying in Florida. This was simply a short vacation gone amok.

Yet the idea of turning around and walking away from Lainey Cooper felt . . . wrong. Deep-down, once-in-a-lifetime wrong. But what other choice did he have?

Well, he did have one. It was more in the form of a reprieve than a plan, but he was a desperate man. "I was behind Minerva's counter today because I was listening to her conversation with Betty Louise."

"Tucker, really, I don't care anymore why—"

"No," he said, perhaps more firmly than he'd intended to, judging by her raised eyebrows. All he knew was that letting Lainey walk away was a mistake he'd regret for the rest of his life. Deciding to tell her the whole truth wasn't a solution, but it was, he hoped, a way to keep her around long enough for him to come up with one. "No, you have to listen to me."

"But—"

"Just walk to the park. They have benches there, right? We'll sit and I'll explain everything to you. Then if you want to walk away and never see me again, I'll do my best to accommodate you."

She stared at him as if he'd grown a third eye.

"What?" he asked, resisting the urge to touch his forehead.

She shook her head slightly. "Nothing. It's just that I've never seen you so . . ."

"Serious?"

"Yes. Exactly."

"Trust me, I can be as serious as a heart attack."

"Shh," she said with a hint of her wry grin. "Those are fighting words in this neck of the woods."

Tucker found himself smiling. She delighted him. He wanted to grab her and kiss her, hold her close and beg her to stay with him while he figured out what he was going to do with his life. He wanted to talk it over with her, find out what she wanted in life, see if there was a way they could blend their two plans together.

"Are you okay?"

"What?" It was his turn to shake his head. "Fine. I'm fine." *Or I will be as soon as I figure out how to keep you from leaving me.* "Listen, will you come to the park, talk with me?"

She looked at him closely. He'd have given a large sum of money to know what she was thinking. But when she nodded in agreement, he didn't care. She wasn't leaving yet. For now, that was enough.

They completed their walk to the park at something faster than a stroll but not quite a dead run, with Tucker urging her on this time. He didn't want to take any chances of her changing her mind. Which was also why he kept his hands to himself.

He ran a quick gaze over the park, the sumptuous landscaping, the winding paths, the large white gazebo positioned in the center, where he imagined evening concerts were held as the sun set over the dazzling expanse of the gulf laid out before them. He zeroed in on the first empty bench he saw and headed in that direction.

As soon as they were seated, he turned, facing her, locking his gaze with hers. He might as well start at the beginning. "I'm not really a masseur," he said without preamble.

Her face paled, leaving bright spots of color blotching her cheeks. "Wha—what?"

She started to rise and he reached out to stop her. "Lainey, wait, let me ex—"

She yanked her arm out of his reach and stood, eyes blazing as she looked down at him. "Why in the hell didn't you tell me this back in front of the café? You could have saved us both some time." She stepped back and raised her palm when he began to rise. "I was wrong. You are another lousy decision." She rolled her eyes and let out a short, humorless laugh. "Boy, can I pick 'em or what?" She looked back at him. "You know, I could have you arrested for impersonating a . . . a . . ."

"Service professional?"

Her eyes narrowed dangerously. "Don't you dare condescend to me. I could sue your nice tight butt all the way to kingdom come and back. How dare you massage me like that!"

"It wasn't very difficult at all, actually." He caught her hand as she swung it at him. "Lainey, let me finish." He had to work harder to hold on to her than he'd expected. She was going to hurt him or herself, so he settled it the only way he knew how. He tugged hard, yanking her off balance. She fell hard against him, landing in a sprawl in his lap. She tried to scramble off him, but he wrapped his arms around her tightly.

Tucker knew he shouldn't be enjoying this. In fact, he could kick his own "tight butt" to kingdom come for handling the situation so badly. But he'd be lying to himself if he said he was upset about where his poor judgment had landed him. Or, more to the point, where it had landed Lainey.

"Let me go," she said, struggling against him. "I'll scream and bring park security down on you so fast—"

"There's no need for that. Stop. If you'll just let me—"

Ow!" She landed a toe to his shin. "Now cut that out before one of us gets hurt." He held her more tightly. She squirmed harder. *Don't think about those soft curves pressed against you.* It was a lost cause. His throbbing shin took a distant second place to the throbbing he was beginning to feel elsewhere.

She all but bared her teeth at him, but she eventually stilled. "Let me go," she said, speaking each word slowly and distinctly. "And I'll forget the whole sordid affair."

He smiled. Bad idea, he realized immediately, and clamped her closer to him. "I'm sorry," he said quietly. "I'm not going to hurt you."

"Too late for that." She twisted around so that she could look straight at him. Her eyes were vivid green— and deadly serious. "Now let me go and I'll promise not to hurt you, either." She nudged her knee, which had somehow made its way up tight between his legs.

"Threat understood," he said. "And believed," he added quickly when she exerted a little pressure. He talked fast. "But if I let you go now, you'll leave without hearing me out. I handled this badly and I owe you an apology, but there is more to the story and it has to do with your aunt Minerva and several of Lillian's clients. You can sue me or punch me or do whatever you think you have to, but first hear me out." She didn't say anything. "Please?"

He wasn't sure whose heart was pounding harder. He deserved the knee in his crotch, and part of him was even proud of Lainey for not surrendering easily. She was more sensible than she gave herself credit for. But there was something in her expression—or maybe he simply wished there was—that told him she wanted to listen to him. He hoped she'd give in to her impulses at least one more time.

"Let me go first."

"But—"

"You want me to trust you? Then you have to trust me."

He eyed her warily.

"Sorry, but it's the best I can do."

"Your best is pretty damn good, Lainey Cooper. Don't let anyone tell you otherwise." He loosened his hold, half bracing himself for a lung-sucking blow between his legs, but she slid easily, if not gracefully, from his grasp and wobbled to a stand.

She folded her arms. "Okay, what's going on?"

"It's not a short story. You might want to sit down."

"I'll sit when I want to. Start at the beginning."

He hid a smile behind his hand—her feet were still well within kicking distance—then rubbed his chin. No matter what anyone said, Lainey Cooper wasn't anybody's fool. "I started at the beginning a few minutes ago. Promise to let me finish this time?"

She merely glared at him.

"Okay, okay. I'll go back a little further. I'm an old friend of Lillian's. In fact, I've known her all my life. She was my mom's best friend. She helped raise me after my mother died."

Lainey instantly sat down next to him, her face wreathed with concern. "Oh, Tucker."

Tucker wanted to shake his head. She was nobody's fool, but she was also a softy. It was hard to believe those caring green eyes had only moments earlier been spitting fire. It was no wonder she got herself into trouble. For all her sensibility and intelligence, she had a heart as big as the moon. He wanted to tell her not to fall for every sad story she heard; he wanted to rail at her to do a better job of protecting that warm, wonderful heart of hers.

He wanted to be the one to protect that heart.

"How old were you?" she asked.

His attention jerked to his knee, where she'd laid her hand over his. "Eight," he answered automatically. Her hand looked small on top of his, yet he felt cared for, protected in a way, by her real and honest concern. Perhaps size had nothing to do with the ability to provide security. Perhaps her heart wasn't the only one that needed protection.

"I'm so sorry," she said. "I lost my folks when I was twenty-five. I can't imagine enduring that kind of loss so young. You still had your father though, right? Did you have any brothers and sisters?"

"No siblings, just me. And, yes, my dad did the best he could for me, but we had a fairly tough time of it. I spent my summers with Lillian until I graduated from high school. My father died of a heart attack a few years after I graduated from college. So Lillian is basically the only family I have."

Lainey sat silently for several moments, then said, "I haven't known Lillian that long, but Minerva has spoken fondly of her since she moved to Sunset Shores about, what, six or seven years ago now?"

"Seven."

She had been staring at their hands but shifted her gaze to his face. "Are you still close? I mean, have you visited Lillian in the last seven years? Because I'm fairly certain Minerva doesn't know anything about you, or she'd have told me when I was talking about you yesterday."

He smiled. "You mean when you were telling her how wonderful my . . . technique was?"

Her skin colored a bit, but then her brow furrowed and any color staining her cheeks at that point was due to anger. "I guess I'd better explain that part next, huh?"

"Do you have any idea how humiliating this is for me? Do you have any idea how hard it was for me to make an appointment, much less see it through once I got a look at you and realized—" She snapped her mouth shut and glanced away.

"Looked at me and what?" Probing was probably not a smart thing to do, but, hell, he hadn't handled anything else real intelligently with her. And besides, he was curious. "Realized what?" He waited, but she didn't look at him. He was at least smart enough to know that touching her could likely cost him the use of a body part or two. "You realized that you were attracted to me and that I was going to be rubbing your body?" he ventured. "There's nothing wrong with that. Hell, I was wondering how in the hell I was going to get through the session without embarrassing myself like a teenager. Why do you think I was so relieved when you decided to call the thing off?"

She looked at him then. "Really? I didn't know. In fact, it was your obvious relief that you didn't have to deal with me that made me decide to stay." She looked down and muttered something under her breath that sounded like "stupid impulses."

Tucker had to curl his fingers into his palms to keep from reaching out and touching her. His resolve lasted about two seconds, but before he could reach for her, she lifted her head and met his gaze.

"Why did you do it? Does Lillian know you're not a licensed masseur?"

"Of course she does. She's the one who asked me to do it."

Obviously confused, Lainey straightened. "Lillian is far too smart a businesswoman to risk a lawsuit or anything else. Why on earth would she ask you to pretend to be a masseur?"

"Because she's worried that your aunt Minerva and two clients of hers, Betty Louise Strickmeyer and a woman named Bernice, are in trouble. Lillian's worried about you, too, Lainey," he said, studying her closely. He was disappointed when she quickly masked her surprise. Her expression grew more shuttered by the second. "She saw Minerva, Bernice, and Betty Louise talking to a strange man in the alley behind the café. She also saw you talking to the same man."

"Tucker, listen—"

"Who is he, Lainey? What's going on?"

SIX

Lainey hadn't expected the tables to be turned on her, much less so swiftly. She needed time to think. Tucker was obviously not happy. Actually, a peek at his face showed he was downright upset.

Information and revelations were swirling inside her head, and she struggled to put them into some semblance of rational order. First and foremost was the fact that Lillian had seen her talking to Damian. Lillian knew that Damian was involved with Minerva, Betty Louise, and Bernice. And Lillian had hired an old friend to play masseur at her salon.

In the face of Tucker's glare, her own eyes narrowed. "Lillian hired you as a spy, didn't she." It wasn't a question. She didn't wait for an answer. She stood, took two steps, then rounded on him. "How dare she! I can't believe she'd stoop so low as to—"

Tucker shot to his feet. "Now hold on there. Lillian does as she damn well pleases, but she didn't stoop to anything other than trying to protect her friends."

As he stormed at her, it occurred to her that Tucker

was even more magnificent when he was being fiercely protective. She spent a second being tempted to tell him that but decided she was too angry at the moment to get any real satisfaction from his reaction. "She has an odd way of showing it," Lainey shot back instead. "Minerva is her closest friend. If she was so worried about what she found out while snooping around the alley, then why didn't she come out and ask her?"

"She was *not* snooping." Tucker stopped and took a visible breath. When he spoke again, his voice was quieter, but there was no mistaking the banked temper behind his suddenly remote eyes. "Lillian would hate being defended this way, and she'd be hurt to think she had to be defended to you at all, but since you're being so hard-headed about this, I'll explain."

Lainey folded her arms and ignored the sting of his well-aimed barb. "Please do," she said coolly. He wasn't the only one who could contain his anger behind icy reserve.

"As I understand it—and I have no reason to question the facts as she told them to me—Lillian went into the alley behind her salon to dump some delivery boxes in the trash and saw Minerva, Bernice, and Betty Louise talking to a man she'd never seen before."

"And from this she created a grand conspiracy?"

"I'm going to ignore that because you're angry with me and because you're scared."

"Scared?" she all but sputtered. But he was way too close to the truth—and she knew she'd only prove it if she argued the point. After a slow, calming breath, she said, "You have no idea what I am feeling at the moment. Finish your story."

He stared at her for another long second, then complied. "She waited for Minerva to mention something about it, but that didn't happen. Lillian figured it was probably someone who was lost and asking for directions. But that didn't explain what Bernice and Betty Louise were doing in the alley with Minerva or why the conversation they were having with the stranger looked more intense than giving directions would necessitate."

She opened her mouth to speak, but he held up a hand. She recrossed her arms and shifted her weight to the other foot, using one raised eyebrow to indicate that he should continue.

"She tried to find out with a few casually asked questions, but still nothing. It bothered her; her intuition was telling her something wasn't right, but she didn't see what else she could do."

"Why didn't she come right out and ask about it?"

"Partly because she wasn't sure what was going on and she didn't want to hurt or embarrass her friends by saying the wrong thing to the wrong person. And partly because she was a little hurt that whatever it was, she hadn't been included." He shrugged, and Lainey detected the smallest hint of a smile ghosting his lips.

Her body leaped in response, which only frustrated her more. What did she have to do? Hit her hormones over their squirmy little heads with a sledgehammer?

"And partly," he continued, "because she loves a good mystery and it was killing her that she couldn't figure this one out."

"So she hired you."

"Not at that point. She had one possible contact left. You."

Lainey blinked but otherwise forced herself not to react. She knew with a certain dread exactly where his story was leading. Damn, damn, damn. This was already complicated enough without Lillian's well-intentioned meddling and her sort-of-nephew's interference.

"She couldn't talk to you around the café, and you weren't a regular salon client. She knew you went to Sam's to buy fish on Saturdays, so she followed you in the hopes of talking to you privately about the whole thing."

And she saw me talking to Damian. Tucker didn't have to finish. "I get the picture."

"Well, would you mind sharing it with the rest of us? She tried to talk to you after the guy left, but you hurried out of there before she could get to you. That was last week. I flew in to see her earlier this week, and she confided the whole thing to me. I'll admit I was skeptical, but we talked and somehow she managed to . . ." His words trailed off, and he shifted his gaze toward a spot on the ground.

It took Lainey a moment of studying him to realize what had stopped his strident speech. "And she snookered you into being a masseur to the seniors in the hopes that while your hands worked them into a state of mindless relaxation, they'd open up and tell you everything."

He lifted his head, his expression aiming for cool nonchalance and missing by a mile. His pink neck told the whole story. She let out a hoot of laughter and clapped her hands together. "A change of careers, huh? Tell me something: Was the rest of the story a setup too? You're really a stockbroker or something, right? Just here on vacation."

"Oh, I was in securities, all right," he said stubbornly, over her laughter, "but not the kind traded on Wall Street."

She sat down on the bench and tried to catch her breath. "Oh, this is almost too ridiculous, even for me." She shook her head and stifled another giggle. "Conrad's mother would have a field day with this one."

Tucker sat down next to her but kept his gaze straight ahead. "Ah, yes, Conrad, the infamous Mrs. Maitland's little golden boy."

Lainey swung her head up, surprised at his sharp sarcasm. His profile was as unrelenting as his determination. His jaw jutted out, under cheekbones cast in stark relief, eyes focused on some faraway point in the gulf.

"You have no idea what kind of man Conrad was." Why in the name of heaven she was defending him, she had no idea. Or maybe it wasn't so much a defense of Conrad as of herself.

"I know he was one of your bad judgments in men," Tucker stated flatly. "And I know Mrs. Maitland is a control freak with more money than common sense. It doesn't take a rocket scientist to add it all up."

"Oh, thanks. Thank you very much." It hurt that he saw so clearly what she had not. It hurt even worse that he apparently thought less of her for her blindness in the matter. But what was most horrifying was that he was capable of hurting her at all. She wasn't supposed to care what Tucker Morgan thought of her. Mrs. Maitland was right, not for the right reasons, but the bottom line was the same. She really was a lost cause.

Lainey sighed and stood. "This has all been so very illuminating, but I really must go now." She half expected him to lunge out and grab her, but he didn't so much as blink when she turned and walked away. That shouldn't have hurt, either.

She'd gone about ten yards or so when he called her name. She stopped but didn't turn.

"Lainey," he said again. He didn't shout. He didn't have to.

After a silent debate, she turned around, but she didn't take a step back in his direction. "What?"

"I quit."

She propped her hands on her hips. "Quit what?"

"Being a masseur-slash-spy for Lillian."

Lainey didn't hide her skepticism. "Have you told *her* that?"

She hardened herself to the smile that struggled and finally broke free, curving his mouth slightly and crinkling the corners of his eyes oh-so-charmingly.

"You can't really tell Lillian anything she doesn't want to hear." His smile faded. "But I knew when you left yesterday that my brief career as a masseur was over."

She took a step closer. "Why?" she demanded. "Was it because you figured I was your ticket to solving the mystery? Is that why you really followed me to Sam's?"

"Solving the mystery was a convenient reason to follow you to Sam's, but I did it because I wanted to see you again. You intrigue me, Lainey. I didn't want you to walk away. I still don't."

"Let's not get into that again." She hoped she sounded strong and sure, because she didn't feel it. She tried to remember all the reasons why she shouldn't care how Tucker Morgan felt about her.

"I also knew I couldn't go on because it wasn't right," he continued. "No matter that Lillian's heart is in the right place. She really is worried about her friends, and she thought she saw a way to help them without hurting anyone. Against my better judgment, I agreed to help her.

I still plan to help, since I'm pretty certain she has good reason to worry."

"You'll help her nose around, just not as a masseur." Her heart told her to share what she knew, join forces. But her head warned her that she was making hasty decisions again, being impulsive. Frustration with him, with the situation and her apparent inability to make a decent judgment on anything, reached maximum load. "So how is she going to explain you to her friends now? A young boyfriend? And what happens when this is over and you visit her the next time? Or did you both figure that maybe after another seven years that anyone who was here during your last visit would either be dead or too senile to remember your face?"

"Don't you think that's a little harsh?"

She did, but until she had time to sort things out, she had to protect herself and, more important, Minerva. Lainey didn't have a handle on how she was going to fix the situation, but involving Tucker could be a mistake on more than one level. If she kept him angry enough at her, maybe he'd give up on grilling her and find his information elsewhere. That thought stopped her cold. Could she risk that alternative?

She wanted to clutch her hair and scream. She hated being indecisive, which was likely how her impulses had grown so healthy and strong. But this time she wanted to be smart, think things through and make the logical, wise choice on how to proceed. She eyed Tucker. His face was a picture of determination. Once again, she didn't think she was going to have the fleeting luxury of time.

And a moment later she was proved right, but not for the reason she'd thought. Tucker was a real problem, but the man she spied walking across the park behind Tucker could prove to be an even bigger one. Damian. If he saw her . . . Or worse, if Tucker saw him and realized who he was . . .

She had to get out of there. Now. "Listen," she said, trying to appear cool and rational. "I'm the last one to judge other people's decisions or how they choose to handle things. But in this case I think you should tell Lillian to stop worrying about it. Things will work out."

"Will they, Lainey? You have to know something of what's going on, and I know you're worried about it too. Do you plan to talk to Minerva about this?"

She worked to maintain eye contact with Tucker and keep Damian's progress in her peripheral vision at the same time. "I'll do what I can, Tucker," she said sincerely. And she would. As soon as she could ditch Tucker and make a beeline for the nearest exit from the park. "You know, we've gotten involved in all of this pretty quickly. I think we ought to back away from it for a while and give them a chance to work things out. Then, if we still think it's necessary, we'll come up with a plan."

Tucker cocked his head to one side.

Damn, she thought, he wasn't buying into it. She swallowed a sigh of impatience.

"Lainey, I really don't see how waiting will help. It may hurt. If you tell me what's going on, maybe I—"

Damian was almost in her direct line of vision. She shifted casually to place Tucker between them, even at the risk of blocking Damian from her sight. Desperate now, she said, "You're right. I—I should. I mean, we should. Talk, that is. Tonight." She smiled too brightly, knowing she was babbling and, gauging Tucker's frown, only raising his suspicions further. "Why don't we meet later tonight and talk? You can pick me up at the café, say around seven-thirty?"

"I can do that, but—"

"Great. Listen, I gotta run. I just remembered something I have to do and . . . well, maybe we shouldn't say anything else until tonight, okay?" She was already backing up.

Tucker folded his arms, his expression more than skeptical. "You promise you'll show?"

She wondered, half hysterically, why her word would mean anything if he didn't trust her, but she nodded. "Promise." She spied a path to her left that led into a landscaped area of dense palmettos and pampas grass, which would provide quick cover. "Tonight, seven-thirty."

She didn't wait for him to answer but turned and made her getaway. She prayed that Damian wouldn't see her, she prayed harder that Tucker wouldn't recognize him as the mystery man. She had no idea how detailed a description Lillian had given him. Damian would blend in fairly well in a general population, but among all these seniors, a long-haired male stood out.

"Lainey," Tucker called out, just as she hit the path. "I won't settle for less than the whole story, including what has you running. That's a promise too."

She didn't answer as she ducked down the path.

Tucker watched her escape. Something had very clearly spooked her. Something . . . or someone. He glanced casually around the park. There were several seniors strolling along the paths and sitting on various benches. He caught a flicker of movement to his left, but it was just someone ducking into the public rest room. He debated whether to check that person out or follow Lainey. Maybe it was another appointment with the mystery man that had her rushing off in a hurry.

Or maybe she just wanted to get the hell away from you, Morgan, and did it the only way she knew how.

He headed toward the path. In his former line of work, he'd had ample cause to learn how to shadow a person inconspicuously. There were many individuals who, for a variety of reasons, required the services of a bodyguard but didn't want anyone to notice the fact. In the last several years, as his business had gone international, he hadn't handled cases personally, spending most of his time in MMSI's various global offices. But some skills, like riding a bike, once learned, stuck with you. And the one he prided himself on was the art of blending in with the scenery.

The path was narrow and curvy with lush vegetation crowding the edges, making it easy to follow without being seen. He jogged slowly, taking the curves carefully until he spied a flash of red and white. He'd found her. He slowed to a walk, confident for the time being that she intended to stay on the path. He wasn't certain how long it winded through the park property, but it seemed to be heading slowly back toward the main street rather than toward the shore. Good. Perhaps she'd leave the park and head back to the café or, better yet, home.

Tucker realized that made no sense. If he truly wanted to solve the mystery, then he should be hoping that she was going to meet the mystery man, not heading home. But there had been something about the way she'd acted before leaving that had made him uneasy. He replayed the scene again in his mind and realized immediately what it was. Fear. There had been a flicker of fear in her eyes as she'd verbally scrambled to get away from him.

He was fairly certain she wasn't afraid of him; she hadn't reacted that way to his parting warning. She hadn't reacted at all. She'd been too distracted.

Tucker was pulled out of his musings when Lainey stopped suddenly and stepped off the path between two spiky palmetto bushes. He barely stopped in time to duck behind the twisted trunks of two palm trees.

Damn. *Where are you going, Lainey?* He waited a few seconds, then crept closer. She pressed on into the narrow strip of lushly designed landscaping that bordered the path. He watched her pick her way around sharp palmetto blades and push past bushy stalks of pampas grass, then stop behind a fat palm at the edge of the carefully tended area. She was scanning the park grounds, particularly the area they'd recently vacated.

Was she checking to see if he was gone? If so, why?

He didn't have to wait long to find out. Apparently satisfied that the coast was clear, Lainey stepped from behind the palm and quickly crossed the manicured park grounds, heading directly back toward the bench they'd shared. Tucker was forced to take up Lainey's hiding place as there was nowhere else for him to hide beyond that point. However, he had a clear view of Lainey's progression.

She surprised him by skirting the bench and heading toward . . . the rest rooms.

"Damn." He should have trusted his initial instincts, but when Lainey Cooper was involved, his gut was invariably so twisted up with her, it lost its ability to guide his judgment. Still, it was just as well he'd taken this route. If she was indeed on her way to meet Mr. X, then utilizing Lillian's description as backup proof, at least he'd know for certain what the guy looked like. He might even be able to tail the guy from the park, find out where he was going, possibly even question him.

Lainey ducked around the back of the small public building and Tucker experienced a moment of doubt. What if the rest room wasn't her destination after all? This time he ignored his twisted gut and used his head. He set out across the grounds, making use of the sporadically placed palm trees and park benches to provide some cover but never losing sight of the small building.

Once there, he edged carefully around the back and peeked around the corner. No sign of her. He swore under his breath as he rapidly scanned the grounds. She was gone. He couldn't see how, even at a run, she could have lost him. Where in the blazes was she? Then he noticed there were two entrances on each side of the facility. It didn't make sense, but it was possible she'd used the other entrance.

A quick check ruled out the men's room. He eyed the curved entry to the ladies' room. Did he dare? The way his luck was going, he'd probably stick his head in the door and give some senior a heart attack. The sound of running feet brought his head up.

He blew out a sigh of disappointment. It was just a jogger. A female jogger. An idea formed. He stepped away from the building intent on getting her attention, but that proved unnecessary when she slowed down and headed for the pedestal-style drinking fountain situated in front of the building.

She was short and trim, with sporty-looking blond hair; obviously younger than the local population by a decade or two. She wore a jade silk jogging jacket over figure-flattering matching green leggings and blindingly white sneakers.

He waited for her to finish, then stepped forward. "Hello."

Startled, she looked up, but her surprise quickly turned into a bright smile and a rapid once-over. "Well, hello, there yourself."

Now that he saw her face more closely, he realized she was closer to Lillian's age than his own. A walking advertisement for the wonders of exercise, he thought, and given her smooth skin, probably cosmetic surgery as well. He wondered if she knew Lillian. Hell, with his luck she was probably her best client.

Tucker groaned at the thought, but time was wasting and he couldn't be choosy. He couldn't cover both entrances, and the longer it took to check the ladies' room out, the better the odds that Lainey, if she was even in there, was long gone.

"I'm Bunny MacAfee," she said, her voice now a soft, low purr. She stepped closer and extended a tanned, perfectly manicured hand, with several glittering rocks adorning her fingers. "And you are?"

Claws and purrs. Just what he needed, a seventy-something-year-old Bunny in a catsuit. "My name is Tucker. Listen, Ms. MacAfee—"

Her smile widened and she sidled closer. "It's Bunny."

He smiled thinly. Why him? "Bunny. Could you do me a favor? I had a little argument with a friend, and she stomped off. I think she's in the bathroom, and I'm wondering if you'd mind checking in there for me to see if she's okay."

Bunny stared at him with avid fascination. "You're new around here, aren't you? I'm sure I wouldn't have forgotten meeting you before."

Great, she wasn't even listening to him. Lainey was likely long gone at this point, and he was stuck trying not to become a scratching post. He took a step back, and she closed the distance between them. "Hey, you know, I'm probably wrong. She probably went straight to the car."

Her eyes glittered. "You need a ride?"

"No! I mean, that's okay. I've got the keys, so she can't go anywhere. She's probably cooled off now." He took several steps back. "Thanks, anyway. Nice meeting you."

"Wait a minute," she said, still ignoring him. She tapped a well-honed claw against her expertly painted lower lip. "Tucker." She snapped her fingers. "You're Lillian's new find, aren't you?" She closed in on him.

He took another step back and came up hard against the stone wall that fronted the rest-room entrance.

"There has been talk, but no one said anything about . . ." She shook her head and looked at him with what Tucker feared was renewed determination. Since she'd already proven she had more determination than the average school of piranhas, it was a scary thought.

A flash of red at the perimeter of the park caught his eye. He was too far away to be sure, but . . .

He took hold of Bunny's shoulders and gently but firmly set her aside. "I think I see her," he said. "I really have to go." He shot her a quick smile of apology, then moved around and away from her at a trot.

"I'll phone Lillian's for an appointment," she called out. "It was a pleasure. Until next week, Tucker!"

He waved over his head without looking back. Over my dead body, he thought grimly. Or over Lillian's. He was definitely no longer in the massage business.

SEVEN

Lainey held a hand to her pounding heart as she continued to tail Damian. She'd originally intended to march straight back to the café and sit Minerva down until the woman listened to what Lainey had to say. She hadn't checked out the hotel, but she knew Damian was in this up to his beady black eyes. He'd been too evasive . . . and too cocky earlier. Then it had occurred to her that maybe cornering Damian on her terms might give her the upper hand for a change.

She had no idea what she was going to say to him when she caught up to him, but she was determined to do whatever she had to, praying madly for divine intervention and inspiration.

She'd almost had a heart attack when she heard Tucker's voice outside the ladies' room. She thought he'd left, but apparently he'd decided to use the men's room. Then she heard the unmistakable voice of Bunny MacAfee and had almost choked on a burst of laughter. She'd almost felt sorry for Tucker. Almost. And, much as she hated the fact, she now owed Bunny one. Lainey knew it would take Tucker no small amount of time to extricate himself from Bunny's clutches, giving Lainey time to make her second getaway from Tucker that afternoon. There would be no escaping a full explanation if he'd caught her back in the park.

Her luck continued on its unprecedented upswing. When she ducked out the other entrance, she spied Damian passing under the wrought-iron archway that formed the side entrance/exit to the park. She'd skirted the building and taken off at a run, putting as many palm trees as possible between herself and the rest rooms . . . and Tucker. But if Bunny was running true to form, she was quite safe.

Damian was now headed toward a quieter street with shops that paralleled the west side of the park. She just had to come up with a plan before he ducked into one of them. She darted a quick look over her shoulder and exhaled briefly in relief. No Tucker.

Then she looked forward . . . and plowed directly into Damian.

"Fancy meeting you here." His heavy sarcasm made it clear that he wasn't the least surprised. She wondered how long he'd known she was behind him.

As usual, he was dressed in black. He'd upscaled the look since college—crisply pleated dress pants, a designer shirt, and leather shoes—but no matter the price tag, his attire still lent an atmosphere of starkness to his already lean, hungry-looking frame. The motif was completed with a tight-to-the-scalp ponytail, a neatly trimmed Fu Manchu–style beard and mustache, all the same shade as the jet-black eyes that always made her feel ill at ease.

"It's a free world last I looked," she said. *Stupid, Lainey. Don't back down.* She'd met Damian in college.

Even on a campus the size of Penn State, almost everyone had known or heard of Damian Winters. He was a certified genius and widely accepted as a certified nut as well. His crazy moneymaking schemes were the stuff of alumni legend. He had made and lost more money than most people saw in a lifetime, all before his junior year. Fortunately for him, his followers had prospered often enough to keep his neck—and his business—intact until he graduated. Though talk of a public lynching was a constant murmur around the quad.

She hadn't kept track of him after graduation and had no idea whether he'd gone on to become a brilliant investment counselor or a brilliant scam artist. And until she'd run into him at Sam's the previous week, she hadn't cared.

"Yes, it is a blessedly free country," he agreed, his smile looking somewhat sinister, bracketed as it was by the Fu Manchu. "So unless you have some specific business you'd like to discuss . . . Or maybe this isn't about business."

Lainey shuddered inwardly as his soulless eyes lit up with an interest that had nothing to do with mutual funds. Funny, she'd never once thought of Damian Winters—when she'd thought of him at all—in a sexual or physical way. It had to be Tucker's influence on her hormones, she decided. When she thought of sex and Tucker, she shuddered, too, although for entirely different reasons.

"It's business," she said abruptly. "I'm still not buying that it's coincidence that you happen to be in Florida."

He shrugged and grinned, suddenly the picture of charming boyish innocence. The transformation was nothing short of astonishing, his gleaming white teeth reminiscent of Tom Cruise's. The result was almost as disconcerting as his more sinister countenance. She had always been amazed that, despite his well-publicized less-than-pristine track record, people willingly funded his latest scheme. Until she saw this face. She couldn't say truthfully what she might have done had he turned this face on her years before. This was the face that made people who should know better part with their money. She knew better than to buy a second of it. At least, thinking of Charlie, she did now.

"People run into folks they haven't seen in years all the time, all over the place. And a whole lot of people went to Penn, Lainey. There is nothing strange about it."

"You're a Philly boy, born and bred," she countered, switching tactics. He sounded quite sincere, and her heart told her, that at least this time, he was telling the truth. Fortunately, she knew better than to trust her heart. "You told anyone who'd listen, and even those who wouldn't, that you'd never leave. What changed your mind? Why Florida?"

"I'm older now, Lainey," he said, a little of the street-smart kid edging into his tone. "Philly is cold. Florida's warm."

"And full of old people with nice fat retirement pensions." Her inference was clear.

He adopted a hurt expression, but Lainey didn't miss the flash of heat in his eyes. She tamped down the renewed urge to rub her arms. There was nothing sexual in those eyes now. The heat came from anger.

"What are you sayin'? You sayin' I'm connin' people here?" As his control slipped, so did his polish. "That I'm a common crook or somethin'? I'm hurt, Lainey."

"One thing you've never been is common, Damian.

Let's just say that finding you residing anywhere near a senior retirement village is a trifle suspect."

The hurt expression subsided, allowing the heat of anger to shine through. She felt scorched. When he stepped closer, it took all her willpower to stand her ground.

He pointed a finger in the air between them, the gesture almost more powerful for the lack of physical contact. "I resent your implication," he said quietly. "And I resent your interference. I'm living here because I like peace and quiet. I'm a businessman just doing his job."

Along with control, his speech had returned to the cultured tones she'd noticed that first day she'd run into him at Sam's. Now, however, they didn't sound so dulcet and smooth; they sounded mechanical, empty, and it made her blood run cold.

"And I'm doing quite nicely, thank you," he continued, his silky tone making her skin crawl. "Now, if you don't have any real business to discuss with me, then I suggest you leave me to mine. Do we understand each other?"

"As long as you understand that Minerva and her friends are to be left out of your latest business proposition. That's the only reason I'm here talking to you."

"Minerva?"

"Minerva Cooper. My aunt. I've never accused you of being dumb, Damian, so don't bother with the clueless routine. I've talked to her, I know she's invested in one of your schemes. Greensleigh Knolls. Does that ring a bell?"

"They're big girls, Lainey. They can make grown-up decisions."

She supposed she should feel relieved that he'd finally admitted it. Instead it made her stomach clench.

"I'd ask why you don't warn your aunt off me," he continued, "but after getting audited for—now what was it? Tax fraud?" He chuckled unkindly. "I don't imagine Minerva is taking investment advice from you these days."

That hurt, not because he knew about it, but because it was the truth. She didn't ask how he'd heard about Charlie. In Sunset Shores, gossip was the world's oldest profession.

"It's hard to make wise decisions when the facts are presented in a way that distorts the risk, Damian. You forget, I've witnessed your convoluted scams, I know how you suck people into investing."

He shrugged, unmoved. "That was more than a decade ago. Things change. I've changed. It's not my fault if people believe what they want to believe. But I guess you know all about that, right?"

"It is if you're telling them what they want to hear when you damn well know it's not what they'll get."

"I never entered into any agreement that I didn't feel would pan out. I'm not stupid, Lainey." She ignored the inference. "They were all legitimate investment ideas."

"Ideas aren't the same as sound business strategies. And pan out for whom? You? I'm sure that is of great comfort to those students who gambled away their college tuition money on one of your sure things. Some of those people were my friends."

"Ah, the great crusader rides to the rescue. I never saw you as the white-charger type, Madelaine Cooper." He folded his arms and settled his weight on his heels. "In fact, if I recall correctly, you used your business degree to marry into Maitland money." He stepped closer, his knowing grin making her stomach roll. "And lost it all too. Philly girl from the southside not good enough to hang with the bluebloods, huh, Lainey? Now you're a divorced waitress dishing out pie to gomers and dating crooked CPAs. Yeah, Lainey, any more brilliant observations you care to dish out along with that pie? You've obviously made so much more of yourself than I have."

His well-aimed attack struck her hard enough to make her feel physically sick, but she used her humiliation to fuel her anger. Hell, it ought to be good for something. "The one thing I learned from the Maitlands is that success isn't measured by your bank balance alone. You could be a multimillionaire for all I know, but you're still a weasel."

His grin widened further as he lifted his shoulders in a careless shrug. "Whatever you say, Lainey. But if I'm a weasel, I'm a rich weasel. And whether or not that makes me successful, I'm happy enough with the wealth."

"Then why don't you buy a yacht and take a long cruise. Go spin your stories of sure things to people who can afford to lose."

"I never promise a sure thing. I've put my business degree to good use over the years."

She didn't let the unspoken dig affect her this time. "I can imagine. Bigger, more complex schemes designed to dupe more money out of more people. No, you're not stupid, Damian. And that's precisely what makes you so dangerous." His eyes narrowed. For a split second Lainey wondered if she were risking more than her pride by provoking him, but she didn't know what else to do. Minerva was convinced that he was the answer to her retirement prayers.

Instead of losing control of his temper, he straightened and moved a step away. "People change, Lainey," he said softly, but the words were as empty and cold as his expression.

She held his gaze. "It's been my experience that most people generally stay the same. The only thing that changes is one's ability to judge their true nature."

His smile made her toes curl until they cramped inside her sneakers. "Good, then we understand each other. Don't mess in my business, Lainey, and I won't be forced to mess in yours."

As before, he gave her no chance to have the last word. He turned and walked away without a backward glance, disappearing around the next corner.

Lainey released a shaky breath.

"I can't decide whether you're incredibly gutsy or incredibly stupid."

Lainey shrieked and spun around. "Tucker!" She clutched her chest, certain her heart was about to burst out of it. "I'd really appreciate it if you'd stop creeping up on me."

He took a step closer, looking as fiercely protective as he had back in the park. Only this time his concern was aimed at her.

"And I'd appreciate you telling me what in the hell is going on around here."

The heat in his eyes was most definitely from anger. So why was her reaction to him completely the opposite of her reaction to Damian? The last thing she felt at the moment was chilled or revolted.

However he affected her, she was still confused and more than a little upset by Damian. Now was not the time to go another round with Tucker. "It doesn't involve you, Tucker. I'm handling it." She tried to shove her way past him, but he grabbed her elbows and held on tight. She couldn't break free, but that didn't stop her from tugging hard. "Bullying me is not going to get you what you want."

He drew her up tight against him, forcing her head back in order to look him in the eyes. "What do you know about what I want?" he asked. The soft menace in his voice and in his eyes should have alarmed her. It didn't.

She trusted him, she realized. He was upset and frustrated, but he would never hurt her.

She looked into his eyes and choked back a semihysterical laugh. *And how the hell would you know, Lainey?* she asked herself in disgust. Damian's barbs had plunged deeper than even he had known, ripping a jagged hole in her nice fantasy that she could truly escape her past, letting all the fears and insecurities she'd neatly tucked away spew forth, overwhelming her. Humiliating her.

And to complete her shameful descent, her eyes burned and filled. She would not cry, not in front of this man. Pouring all of the unvented emotion she had into one balled-up knot of energy, she yanked out of his grip, stumbling backward a few steps when she succeeded. Her hands flew up to ward off his automatic attempt to help.

"Don't touch me, Tucker Morgan. I've been pushed around enough for one day. I'm going home." This time when she walked past him he left her alone. When he silently fell into step beside her, she didn't know whether to scream in frustration or fall into his arms and weep out all of her anger and indecision and self-pity. Neither was acceptable, so she pulled herself together and continued walking in silence.

He remained silent, matching his pace to hers, giving her much-needed time to work things through in her head. His big, solid body and quiet confidence provided a surprisingly deep sense of comfort. It was deceptively simple, she thought as they crossed in front of the park and headed up Main Street toward the café. Sort of like a big brother who was smart enough to let his sister fight her own battles, but loyal enough to make sure she got home safely.

But that analogy wasn't quite right. He made her feel many things, none of them sisterly. So what category did her feelings fall into? Her head kept casting him as an opponent, yet her heart staunchly maintained that he was an ally. Why couldn't she trust her heart and ask him to help her? Was it his motives she suspected? Or her own judgment? And why in the hell was she thinking about Tucker when she should be thinking of some way to intervene in Damian's scheme without jeopardizing her health or anyone else's? Her steps slowed as that last part sunk in.

Until that afternoon she'd only considered Damian fiscally dangerous. Would he actually harm one of them? Back there on the sidewalk she'd been thinking of her own skin, but it occurred to her now that there was a much easier way for him to get to her than a direct threat. No, she thought immediately, he wouldn't go that far. His forte was smooth talking, not bone breaking. She doubted he had changed in that respect. Even so, she stopped, her skin clammy and cold despite the warm, muggy afternoon air.

There was a sigh of impatience, then a very quiet "Let me help you."

A gentle touch on her shoulder brought her head up.

"He's never been the violent type. I don't think he'd hurt one of them. Do you?" she asked, and in doing so she realized she had made her decision. She was asking for help. She was going to trust him. At least this far.

Tucker didn't need to ask her to explain. He'd overheard enough of her conversation with Damian to have a clear idea of what had made her skin all clammy and her face lose its color. It had finally occurred to her that she wasn't the only one who could get hurt. Letting her come to that conclusion on her own when he wanted to shake it into her had been one of the hardest things he'd ever done. And looking into her eyes, her trusting eyes, the most worthwhile too.

"As you said back there, he's not stupid." He wanted to stroke her, to see the color come back into her skin, the impulsive spark leap in her eyes. He stuck his hands in his pockets. "I doubt he'd risk whatever he has cooked up by harming a potential investor. But he's smart enough to try to make you believe he might if he thinks it will get you to back off until he's done working his scam."

"It *is* a scam, Tucker." Her eyes were bright now, but with desperation. As if she thought he wouldn't believe her.

"I think so too," he said truthfully. It was the right thing to say. She relaxed, albeit slightly. He couldn't stand it; he slipped his hands free and held one out to her. "Walk. Next to a long drive on a winding country road, it's the best way to clear the cobwebs and think." He waited an eternal heartbeat, then she slid her hand into his. He noticed she didn't look at him as she turned and they began walking. He didn't mind. Her hand was warming in his. It was a good start.

"Weasels like Damian are pretty easy to spot but also slippery to catch."

"Then why doesn't Minerva see—" She broke off, and a quick glance showed that bright spots of color had returned to her cheeks.

He gave her hand a gentle squeeze and wondered again at the deep, abiding need he seemed to have to care for and protect her. These feelings weren't remotely professional; in fact, they were more intensely personal than anything he'd ever felt before. "Professional" also didn't describe the things he would very much like to do to Damian if he ever caught the man so much as breathing in Lainey's direction again.

It had taken incredible restraint not to step out of the shop doorway he'd ducked into and pound Damian's smirking million-dollar smile down his slick, little weasel throat. If it hadn't ended when it did, he'd no doubt be explaining himself to the local police right about now. But if he expected her to trust herself, he had to trust her too.

"Don't blame your aunt, Lainey." When she stiffened, he rubbed her knuckles with his thumb and kept them moving at a slow but steady stroll up Main. "And don't blame yourself."

"She won't listen to me." She let out an empty laugh that made his heart ache. "I can't blame her. Damian is right. Who am I to judge?"

Tucker stopped abruptly and turned her to face him. "Lainey—"

But instead of the self-pity he'd expected to see, her face was a mask of determination. "She thinks I'm oversensitive because of what happened with Charlie. But I'm right this time, Tucker. I know it. Damian knows it too.

He's probably laughing himself silly right this minute. What am I going to do?"

With one finger he caressed her cheek, then tilted her tight jaw up. "Did it ever occur to you that there might be nothing you can do?"

"No." Her tone brooked no argument. "I can't let her throw away her money. Not when I know—"

"She *is* an adult. It is her decision. You can make her aware of Damian's past and that may change her mind. Or it might be too late even if she wanted to. He's very likely got her signature on something, if not a check. He's not going to walk away from a sure thing, either. He'll do whatever he thinks he has to, to persuade her he's the real deal."

She moved her chin away from his touch. "I thought you wanted to help me." Her eyes were accusing; her tone made it clear she felt betrayed.

It angered him that she thought he should be added to the list of people who'd let her down. But what reason had he given her to think otherwise? He'd charmed, bullied, and demanded . . . and when she'd finally turned to him, his first bit of advice had been for her to walk away from her newly trusted instincts. It wasn't what he'd meant, it had merely been a starting point to looking at the full range of possibilities, but that meant little now.

And she thought *she* was a screwup with relationships. He felt like the prize champ. Chump was more like it.

"I seem to be the one who needs to think things out first. I'm not going about this right. I do want to help, Lainey," he stated firmly. "And I will."

Her eyes narrowed. "For Lillian? Or because you think we can make a difference?"

"No," he said immediately. "Not just for Lillian. Get

this straight. I care about you, Lainey. A great deal. I think you are a warm, caring, sweet, impulsive woman who doesn't wait for life to come to her but goes out after it. If someone you care about is hurting, you hurt. If you see a way to fix something, you jump in and try to fix it." He held up his hand to stall her retort.

She clamped her mouth shut, but her eyes were still shooting sparks of defiance.

"And sometimes when you care you make hasty decisions or jump in too quickly and it snaps back and bites you." The defiance was quickly tinged with hurt. He stepped closer but still did not touch her. "You're not the only one, Lainey. Sure we sometimes wish we'd handled things differently in retrospect. I wish I'd handled things with you differently. It doesn't make them bad character traits, any more than it makes us bad people for having them. They're what makes you who you are. And you're a wonderful person, Lainey Cooper. Don't be so hard on yourself."

She crossed her arms. "You don't fight fair," she said stubbornly, but the daggers, both of defiance and pain, were gone from her eyes.

"I don't want to fight at all."

"You also have a twisted way of making an apology, assuming that if I am not hard on myself, I'd be a hypocrite to be hard on you for making the same mistakes."

He smiled. "I hadn't planned it that way, but since you mentioned it . . ."

"I'm not sure on either score," she said sincerely. "I'll let you know."

"Understood. Thinking things out isn't a bad way to go when you have that luxury. I do want to help you."

"How? By making me walk away from the whole

thing and stand by while Minerva gambles away a goodly chunk of her life's savings? I'm sorry, I can't do that."

"Slow down a second. I only pointed that out because it needed saying. You need to understand all the possibilities before you can plan the most effective strategy. And one of those possibilities is that nothing we do or say will stop this from happening. In the end, it is her decision. You have to face that, deal with that first."

Her expression fell; her shoulders slumped. "You're right." Her voice was low. "I just want to do the right thing for once."

He did touch her then, a whisper of a caress over her hair and down her cheek. "Lainey, look at me."

She did. The glassy sheen of her eyes made his heart ache.

"We'll figure something out." He'd never meant anything more in his entire life. First he had to erase those tears. He let a small smile kick up the corners of his mouth. "I can always break Damian's kneecaps, if that would make you feel better. I know it would make me feel better."

She laughed and sniffed at the same time. "If I thought it would stop him, I'd take the first whack."

"You have no idea how hard it was for me to stand there and listen. I—"

Color flooded her face. "You heard it all?" She waved her hand. "Never mind. What's a little more humiliation?"

"What is there to be humiliated about? You made some decisions that didn't turn out so well. Madelaine Cooper isn't perfect. Who is?"

"It's more than that, Tucker. I jump first, think about the consequences second. Most people learn from their mistakes, but I seem destined to make mine over and over." Her lip trembled as she looked at him again. "I've made a mess out of a lot of things in my life. Even coming to Florida was a way to escape things that were getting too hard to deal with. Since I've gotten here I've tried to think more responsibly, act after giving a situation a thorough going-over. And then along comes Charlie, and I think I'm being nice to the twins by seeing him, and he turns out to be a nice guy, very low-key. Everything about him screamed safe. So I jump at his very nice and low-key offer to help invest my money. And I almost land in jail. The IRS will be paying close attention to me for years. I'm a business major, for goodness' sake, and I couldn't see through tax fraud."

"Maybe you saw what Charlie wanted you to see, a nice man who was trying to help a newly single woman expand her investment base. Weasels come in all shapes and colors, Lainey. You can't spot them all."

"So what was my excuse with you?" She blushed but kept her chin tilted in determination. "I made the appointment, again for the twins, although I had no idea they were matchmaking. And even when I knew I was in trouble—"

"Trouble?"

She glanced down, then back up, a half-smile darting around her mouth despite her embarrassment. "Let's just say I was already a bit uncomfortable with the whole idea, and my immediate reaction to you didn't exactly make me feel more secure."

Tucker grinned, scooped up her hand, and resumed their walk. In silent agreement, at the first corner they turned right, away from Main street and the café. "Continue. I'm liking this conversation."

"I'll bet." She was silent for a few seconds, and he was about to tell her to let it go, but then she continued. "Anyway, I was all set to get the hell out of there, but you looked so damned relieved that I—"

"Slid onto my massage table and almost made me explode. Do you have any idea what you in that towel were doing to me?"

She smiled, her cheeks pink, but her eyes were gleaming. "Thank you. But it still doesn't change the fact that I acted on impulse. Again."

"Well, you were hardly in danger of being hurt or hurting anyone else. I don't think getting a massage qualifies as a mistake."

"It's symbolic of my personality, Tucker. It's proof I haven't changed."

"I still don't see why you think you should."

She sighed. "Well, I do. My reasons for coming to Florida might not have been the most admirable, but I've found a home here, a place where I feel I belong, with people I care about and who care about me. And now something is happening that can hurt the people that mean the most to me. I can keep that from happening. I need to. It's the responsible thing to do, Tucker."

"Tracking Damian down and confronting him isn't the responsible way to handle this."

She pulled him to a stop. "And going undercover as a masseur is?"

"Touché," he said with a smile. "But that proves my point. We do what we think is right, and sometimes, when our hearts are involved, we don't think clearly in our rush to help." He stepped closer to her. "Trust me, I get within ten feet of you, and my brain turns to mush.

The harder I try to get you to trust me, the harder you push me away."

She didn't say anything at first. He watched her wet her lips. He bit his to keep from kissing her.

"I wanted to do this on my own," she said finally. "I need to learn to trust myself again first. You're right, confronting Damian might not have been the smart thing to do. But I'd already talked to Minerva, and she's not budging. I didn't see that I had any other avenues."

"So I'm a last-ditch effort?"

She sighed heavily. "I don't know what you are."

"Ouch." He rubbed a hand over his heart. "At least you're honest."

"I'm not trying to hurt you, Tucker. See what I mean? I can't even ask for help without bumbling it." She blew out an exasperated breath and looked away.

"Lainey."

"What?" She didn't look at him.

"You want my help but not me."

She turned to him. "That's not entirely true. I like you, Tucker. I'm attracted to you. I won't even discuss what I want because your head would just swell up." At his wide grin she blushed hotly. "Don't *even* go there," she warned.

He raised his hand. "Not me. Scout's honor."

"You were never a scout."

"How can you be so sure?" he said, looking wounded. When she merely raised an eyebrow, he relented. "Okay. See, you can, too, judge men."

She rolled her eyes. "Only you can turn everything into a life lesson for Lainey."

"Just trying to help."

She grew serious. "Can you? Just help, I mean?"

"If that's all you want, yes."

"It's all I can handle right now." There was honest pain shadowing her eyes.

"Then that's all you'll get. Right now."

EIGHT

"I think Lillian will be more than pleased." Tucker shook Stephan's beefy hand and handed him one of Lillian's salon cards. "I'll tell her to expect your call." The hulking Swedish masseur nodded, then disappeared into the men's locker room.

Quite pleased with himself, Tucker strolled across the Fairmont Hotel lobby and made himself comfortable in one of the deeply cushioned loveseats. He kept his eyes on the entrance's revolving doors. Lainey was due any second. They'd parted that afternoon on the agreement to meet for dinner and a discussion regarding the situation with Damian and hopefully find some solutions. Tucker had put the intervening time to good use. Excellent use, he thought, allowing himself a smug smile. He'd spent a good deal of the time on the phone in his room, tracking down people who might be able to help him get more information on Mr. Damian Winters and the Greensleigh Knolls project. He'd also contacted one of his former clients who happened to be an international investment broker.

Tucker had been so flush with his success rate, he'd decided to go for broke and solve his dilemma on how to end his employment at Lillian's salon. His smile grew to a grin as he imagined Lillian's reaction to his replacement. Yes, he'd had quite a day.

A flash of green caught his eye. Lainey. She pushed through the doors and all thoughts of Stephan massaging Lillian's blue-hairs fled as he watched her stop and scan the crowded lobby. Her hair was sexy, all wavy and wind-tossed. His fingers curled with the need to touch her. She wore a jewel-green tank-top dress that hugged her slight curves and bared enough leg to make him swallow hard and shift in his seat.

All his accomplishments shrank to a minuscule pile of nothing when stacked against the one accomplishment he'd yet to achieve: finding a way to earn Lainey Cooper's full and complete trust. And if he somehow managed that miracle, he'd go for broke again and shoot for the big prize: capturing her heart. In the time since he'd sold MMSI, his plans had been vague at best, but he'd assumed he'd figure out new career and location first, then start working on friends and, if he was lucky, family.

It wasn't happening quite the way he'd planned. His new life was planning itself. He had to decide to play or pass.

Tucker Morgan wanted to play.

He allowed himself the additional aching treat of watching Lainey turn in a slow circle as she continued to look for him, then he stood while he could still do so and retain his dignity and waved. "Over here."

She turned, immediately spied him, and smiled. His heartbeat sped up and his pulse throbbed. As she walked toward him, he thought how wonderful it would be to wake up to that smile every morning and come home to it every night. Yes, he definitely wanted to play. And when he played, he played for keeps.

"Hi, I didn't see you," she said.

"I was practicing being a superspy."

Her skin was a little flushed from the evening humidity, her eyes sparkled, her smile was sincere. Just friends, he reminded himself. He'd keep his hands off her—for now—if it killed him. He gestured to the garden restaurant located in the atrium, which was visible at the top of the floating central staircase. "Shall we?" With a quick nod, she proceeded him up the stairs. Watching the quiet sway of her delectably showcased hips, he gripped the gold-plated handrail to keep from grabbing her and thought he'd be lucky to make it through appetizers.

He'd reserved a private table in the outside patio garden overlooking the gulf. "Is that okay with you? It should cool off soon, and I understand the sunset view is not to be missed."

Her smile faltered a bit, but he kept his firmly in place. He wanted to play, but that didn't mean he had to play fair.

"Sounds nice," she said with just a touch of cool reserve.

"I thought it would give us some privacy." At her questioning look, he added, "Considering the topic under discussion, I thought keeping a low profile was a good idea."

"You're probably right." Her expression smoothed, but there was a wariness shadowing her eyes now. He wasn't sure if it was the mention of their reason for being there or because she doubted his sincerity. Probably a little of both, he thought.

They were seated in a small alcove with ferns and tropical flowers providing a subtle screen from neighboring tables. Bougainvillea and clematis trailed along the balcony railing, and beyond that all that was visible was the sparkling sun-tipped waters of the gulf.

"Nice place," she said as she slid her linen napkin from her plate.

"You've never eaten here?"

She laughed. "It's a little steep for me. You're staying here?"

He smiled at her skeptical tone. "For the time being." Now was not the time to mention the real estate agent he'd also spoken to that afternoon.

"You must have guarded some fairly exclusive bodies." She smiled apologetically. "Sorry. That was tacky of me."

He shook his head, thinking he'd actually enjoy talking about his former profession with her. "If by exclusive you mean demanding, overbearing, and generally pains in the rear, then yes, that defines my former clientele pretty well."

"Is that why you quit? You didn't enjoy it?"

"I didn't say that."

She smiled. "Which part?"

"Both. I loved my job. In fact, it was my whole life. Which is why I no longer do it. I ran my own company with a friend. He died several months ago from a heart attack. After that, I sold it."

"I'm so sorry," she said quietly. "Please don't feel like you have to—"

"No, I don't mind. In fact, other than a brief interrogation by Lillian, I haven't really talked about it to anyone."

"I'm all ears."

Not hardly, he thought, fighting to keep his eyes on hers and off the soft curve of her lips, her slender neck, and the sweet slope of her tanned shoulders. He stopped doing inventory and pulled his thoughts back to the topic at hand. Her expression told him that she was serious about wanting to listen. And that was a good thing, because he had an undeniable need to tell her . . . everything.

"It was at Pete's funeral—Peter Manning was my partner. Anyway, he was a year younger than me. Thirty-eight."

"So young. That's terrible. Did he have a family?"

Tucker shook his head. "The company was our family. It was our everything. I stood there in the cemetery with a roll of antacids in my pocket and a grinding headache and I realized that I wasn't very far from finding myself right where he was."

"So you just up and sold it? It must have been difficult."

"I think quitting a lifelong smoking habit cold turkey would have been easier." He paused and stared out over the water, watching the gold light begin to blend in at the horizon with shades of rose and purple. "I loved what I did."

"It shows. Your eyes take on this sort of . . . I don't know . . . gleam when you talk about it. Do you regret your decision?"

"No," he said immediately. "I know I did the right thing."

"Couldn't you have scaled back or something? Done the job on a more moderate level?"

"Not the way it was, no. We started about sixteen

years ago, right after college. Pete and I went to school together, and to make money we moonlighted as bouncers at the campus club. Being business majors . . ." He broke off and grinned. "Something you might know a little about."

"Somehow I think the similarity begins and ends right there, but go on."

"Anyway, we had other local clubs asking us to work part-time, so we came up with the idea of starting a bouncer business. One thing led to another and . . ." He shrugged. "It sort of took on a life of its own. We both took some extra courses in security training along with some martial arts–related training, and after graduation we decided to go into business full-time. We poured our hearts and souls into it, but we loved every minute of it. It took off amazingly quickly, and before we knew it, we were getting calls to provide bodyguard service for some local politicians and other business bigwigs. After a couple of years, Pete had developed some contacts overseas through one of our German clients, and we eventually opened a branch office in Europe. It sort of mushroomed after that."

Lainey had propped her chin on one hand, her gaze rapt on his.

He smiled sheepishly. "And now I'll shut up."

She didn't move other than to speak. "Don't. I think it's interesting. I bet you have some amazing stories."

"One or two."

"I'd enjoy hearing them sometime."

Tucker's smile faltered. Her expression was completely sincere and totally without guile. Did she have any idea how badly he wanted to share a whole lot more than his past exploits? "Anytime," he said, striving to sound casual.

They both saw the approaching waiter. She sat up and folded her hands in her lap. "Whenever you're back in town," she added quickly, then turned to their server with a smile and gave her drink order, effectively ending the conversation.

So much for new hopes. Tucker ordered an iced tea through almost gritted teeth. When the waiter left them, he blindly shifted his attention to his menu.

Before he could decide how best to proceed, the waiter returned, and they spent several minutes making their dinner decisions. When they were alone again, Lainey solved the problem by speaking first.

"So I guess this isn't the vacation you planned, huh?"

If you only knew. "Not exactly. Which is why I usually fly Lillian to meet me. I have a slightly greater chance of controlling the situation that way."

Lainey's eyes lit up, and she tapped her forehead. "Duh. I just realized you're the 'family' she visits on her annual exotic vacations. Her ladies drool over them, you know. I think it's sweet that you do that for her."

"Self-protection. Strictly self-protection."

Lainey chuckled. "I'm not sure even an international crew of bodyguards could provide ample protection from Lillian if she has her mind set on something. You're lucky you only ended up as a masseur."

He watched, totally enthralled by the way her cheeks pinkened.

"Your eyes are doing that gleam thing again," she said. "I don't even want to know what you're thinking this time."

No, you don't, Lainey, he silently agreed. *Because if I told you I was thinking how much fun it will be to tell our grand-children we met at a massage parlor, you'd run and never look back.*

He let her off the hook. "Well, I think I solved that particular employment problem before you arrived."

"You found yourself a replacement Lillian will approve of? How did you achieve that minor miracle?"

"The Fairmont has a wonderful masseur named Stephan. He's a giant of a Swede with the hands of an angel. I asked him if he knew of anyone who might fit the bill at Lillian's, and he said he was only working here part-time and might be interested in doing it himself." Tucker grinned. "At least I'm pretty sure that's what he meant. He understands English but speaks next to none. If his appearance doesn't give Lillian's ladies heart attacks, I think he'll be a big hit. 'Big' being the key word here. Lillian met him a few days ago when she was here looking for me. Let's just say I think she'll approve."

Lainey was laughing hard at this point and finally raised her hand. "Stop. The visual alone is killing me." She took a sip of water, then caught his eye and giggled again. "Oh, Tucker, if I didn't know Lillian, I'd say you should be ashamed of yourself. But you just know she'll love the idea."

"I'm counting on it. I bruise easily."

She took another sip, then leaned back. "You know, I was really nervous about tonight. I'm not anymore. Thank you for that, Tucker." Her smile faded, but her eyes stayed soft and unwary. Tucker wished like hell he could keep them that way. But as much as he wished this was a purely social occasion, it wasn't.

"Nothing to thank me for."

"Not true, but I won't argue the point. I guess we should talk about the reason we're really here."

Tucker judiciously decided not to respond to that remark.

"I had hoped to talk to Minerva this afternoon, but she was gone when I got back. Did you find out anything about Damian or Greensleigh?" she asked.

He watched her run a finger around the edge of her glass, his stomach clenching as her finger rubbed past the spot where she'd left a light lipstick mark on the glass. He pulled his gaze to hers and reluctantly focused on business. He'd deal with the pleasure part later.

"I made a few calls to some of my former clients, one of whom is involved in international investments. He had some interesting information."

"On Damian? Somehow I never thought of Damian as being savvy enough for the international market." She gestured to the quiet development sprawling along the coastline. "This is more his speed."

"Well, it seems he's worked in Mexico and the Caribbean, or at least he's sold shares in a development supposedly taking place there."

"You lost me."

"You're right when you say senior villages are Damian's speed. In fact, they are his specialty, at least they seem to be from the little bit I learned. My client was working on a resort venture in Barbados that was linking with another resort planned for the west coast of Mexico. During his dealings in obtaining investors, he heard a rumor that someone purporting to be part of his investment team was selling shares in a supposed planned senior village that would be part of these resorts."

"Supposed village? Meaning he was using the resort

investment portfolio to get unsuspecting seniors to invest in a bogus senior vacation-type village, saying it was going to be part of the resort."

"You catch on quick."

She pushed her glass away. "I wish I didn't. I assume this person was Damian."

"Can't say for sure. He split before the authorities could track him down. But from what my client learned, it sure sounds like him."

"So what does that mean? Do we go to the police?" She waved a hand. "On second thought," she said dryly, "Roscoe Tumble might not be a real asset here."

"Hey, don't sell old Tumbleweed short."

"You know Roscoe?"

"Let's just say I've intervened on Lillian's behalf in some . . . ah, interactions she's had with the city government and the sheriff's department."

Lainey laughed. "I don't think I want to know."

"You're right," Tucker said, smiling. "But Lillian made me promise not to involve the sheriff because she doesn't want to chance embarrassing Minerva in such a public way."

Lainey leaned forward. "I think that's sweet of her, but maybe a little shortsighted. Minerva will be hurt a whole lot worse if Damian scams her and the other two ladies out of their retirement funds."

Tucker sighed. "I explained the same thing to her, but she was adamant." He raised his hand to stall her response. "If there doesn't seem to be another more discreet way to handle things, then we'll call Roscoe. I won't let Minerva or her friends get hurt, Lainey."

She held his gaze for a moment. "Thank you," she said quietly. She fussed with the rim of her water glass again, then looked at him. "And thank you for all you're doing to help Lillian help Minerva. I know you probably want to get back to wherever it is you're from—"

"Seattle."

Her eyes widened. "Seattle?"

He smiled. "What's wrong with Seattle?"

"I don't know. Nothing. I guess it is coastal and lets you hop around the world and all, but . . . I guess I just didn't picture you . . . I don't know . . ."

"How *do* you picture me, Lainey?"

She toyed with the stem on her glass, straightened her flatware, then turned her attention to the gulf as the last sliver of sun dipped below the horizon.

"Lainey?"

She finally looked at him. "I try not to picture you at all."

"Why is that?" he asked, proud of his even voice, though his heart felt as if all the lifeblood was pumping out of it.

She folded her hands in her lap but held his gaze. "Because wherever or however I might think of you, the reality is, it can't include you being here, so why bother?"

"I am here."

"For now."

"For now is all I have. I sold my business on a lightning-fast decision. I had no big plans, no new career in mind, but I did it because my gut and my heart told me that if I didn't want to end up like Pete, if I wanted a life that included something more than a job, it was jump now or go down with my ship. I still have no plans. I came here to see Lillian and to spend some time letting the sun soak into my skin while I figure out what the hell I want to do with the rest of my life."

She folded her arms, her posture seemingly relaxed, but the jut of her jaw was telling another story. "What the hell do you want to do, Tucker?"

He held her gaze and told her the truth. "I want friends who aren't also my clients. I want a job that ends at some finite point each day. I want a place to live that is a home and not just a mailing address." He paused and cleared his suddenly tight throat. "I want a family. I want balance." He forced himself to finish despite the fear and wariness growing steadily in her eyes with each word he spoke. "And I want you. It's backwards and not planned or even sensible given where I'm at in my life, but none of that seems to matter. I want you, Lainey."

The waiter chose that monumental moment to appear, wielding a huge tray filled by their dinner entrées, which shielded him from Lainey's reaction. Tucker gave serious thought to tossing the guy over the balcony but managed to restrain the urge at the last moment. The young man apparently sensed the tension and quickly dispensed their meals and beat a hasty retreat.

Lainey's attention was focused exclusively on her shrimp scallopini. Tucker moved his mahimahi around on his plate and debated which approach to take. His head was telling him to demand an honest response, but his heart was busy building a nice high wall to hide behind and was perfectly content to let the discussion pass without further comment.

He watched from the corner of his eye as she sipped her wine, then gave up trying to eat and stared openly at her.

"It's very good," she said, not looking up. "How is yours?"

He couldn't do this, couldn't pretend he hadn't laid

his heart on the table. He'd taken the biggest risk of his life by selling his business. What was the point of it if he wasn't willing to pursue the very thing he'd sold it to have?

"I couldn't say. I seem to have more important things on my mind at the moment. I sort of thought you might have something else you'd like to discuss." He watched her spear another piece of shrimp. He thought he might scream in frustration, or at least throw her shrimp over the gold-plated handrail, but before he exploded, she placed her loaded fork on the plate and looked up at him.

"So much for the just-friends idea, huh?" Her attempted smile faded quickly. "I don't know what to say to you, Tucker."

"I'm thoroughly enjoying our friendship, Lainey. But I can't seem to stop wanting more. I don't want to stop."

"And then what?" she asked. She lifted her hand. "Don't answer that. Tucker . . ." She broke off on a sigh.

"Do you want me, Lainey?"

She jerked her gaze to his; even in the waning light he could see the heat lighting her cheeks.

"Do you want me?" he repeated.

"It's not about what I want."

"Then what the hell is it about? And don't give me this stuff about impulses and bad choices in men. You're an intelligent, caring woman who can make her own decisions."

Her eyes flashed as she pressed one balled-up hand on the table. "And what if I *decide* not to choose you? What if I *decide* that I don't want to wait around while you find yourself on the off chance that I'll be part of that grand plan? And here's a stunning thought: What if I don't have to tell you why I made that choice? What if I told you that it's none of your business why I do what I do?"

"What if you just decide to tell me the truth?"

She threw her napkin on the table and scooted from her seat. "What if I decide to tell you to go to hell?"

He snagged her arm as she tried to pass him. "Don't leave."

She glared down at him. "Don't order me around."

He let go and she stomped off. Swearing, he tossed some bills on the table between their plates of uneaten food and took off after her.

He caught up to her as she sailed out of the revolving doors.

"Grab me again and I'll scream," she warned him.

He held his hands palms up. "Do you need a ride?"

She looked at him as if he'd lost his mind, then turned away and started up the street, away from the shoreline toward the center of town.

He fell into place beside her, wondering how she managed to keep such a fast pace in heels. "We still need to talk about Damian."

"We don't need to talk about anything. I'll take care of Damian. Minerva is my aunt and my concern."

"Why are you running, Lainey?"

"To get away from you?" she said sarcastically.

"I mean figuratively. What are you so afraid of? What is it that you think will happen if you're honest with me about how you feel?"

She stopped abruptly and faced him, hands planted on her hips. "Why is it that if a woman doesn't fall all over a guy because he's deigned to admit he wants her, it means she's running from something? Did it ever occur to you that maybe I just don't want you back?"

"No."

Her eyes popped wide and her mouth opened and shut like a fish's. If he hadn't felt as if the rest of his life was on the line, he might have laughed. As it was a hint of a smile teased his tightly pressed lips. Her eyes narrowed dangerously.

"Why, you pompous, conceited—"

"You want me back, Lainey."

"Egotistical, self-centered, bullying—"

"You want me bad. You told me so. You've wanted me ever since you laid eyes on my—what did you call it? My tight butt?—so don't get all holier-than-thou on me because I'm being honest. You're running, Lainey. Flat-out, dead-run, hightailing it."

Her expression faltered and her arms crept across her stomach, where she folded them like a protective shield.

"And if all I wanted was you on your back for a quick fling before I flew off to 'find myself,' then I gotta tell you, you're too much work." He raised his hand when her mouth dropped open again. "But that's not all I want. And because it's not all I want, I'm busting my chops doing anything I can to keep you from walking away from me. And I'll continue to bust them until you tell me why it is you won't give me—us—a chance." He realized he was shouting and made a conscious effort to lower his voice. He stepped closer and was heartened when she didn't move away or, worse, slug him. She was looking sort of lost and shell-shocked at the moment, and he couldn't stand there and yell at her any longer.

"Lainey," he said softly. She looked down at her feet, then at some vague point past his shoulder. He reached out and stroked her cheek, then her chin. She didn't step away, so he did it again, pushing a stray curl from her face. "Instead of running away from me, why don't you try running to me? I'm right here. And as long as you're here, I'm not going anywhere." He gently but firmly turned her face to his. "I don't want to fight you. I want to make love to you. With you."

She stilled. "You don't even know me, Tucker. Not really."

He stepped closer. "I know enough."

"No, you don't. You don't know what's inside me, inside my head and my heart."

He closed the remaining distance between them. "Then why don't you tell me so I do know?" Her eyes were eloquent pools of restrained need, filled with confusion and pain. His heart had become a tight ball of fear and anxiety, but he slowly allowed it to expand. "Why don't you tell me about your bad decisions so that I know how to make you understand I'm not one of them?" He lowered his mouth closer to hers, dying inside from the almost desperate need to taste her.

"I can't make another rash mistake, Tucker," she whispered. "I won't survive it."

He paused and pulled back enough to look into her eyes. "I'm not a mistake, Lainey, rash or otherwise. If you can't trust me, trust this." He fitted his mouth to hers, gently but not tentatively. He explored with soft kisses, easing her lips apart. At the first touch of her tongue, his body tightened to the point of sublime pain. His pulse sang and his heart pounded furiously inside his chest. Her response wasn't bold or wanton or remotely rash. It was sweet and gentle. . . . It was Lainey.

He pulled her into his arms. She opened her mouth to him, met his increasing urgency with a matching need of her own. "I do know you," he whispered against her lips.

"I know you're mine." Her only response was a tiny moan at the back of her throat as she deepened the kiss, but it was enough to shake him. He felt his control spinning away rapidly.

The quiet clearing of a throat brought him back to earth with a startling thud.

"Don't stare, Matilda, it's rude" came an elderly rasp of a voice.

"It's sweet, Henry. The world needs more of that kind of thing if you ask me."

"I didn't ask. Stop gawking."

Lainey broke contact and pulled away, her face on fire. Tucker worked hard at gathering his control, then reluctantly turned, tucking Lainey protectively under his arm before she could do something foolish, like escape. He nodded his head as the older couple passed them. "Evening," he said between a clenched-jaw smile.

The older woman beamed up at him, her faded eyes twinkling and a becoming blush lighting her cheeks. "Quite a beautiful one," she said, her gaze moving to Lainey, then back to him.

His own smile thawed and became natural. He winked at her. "Why, yes, it most certainly is." He swallowed a chuckle as Henry took a tighter hold of Matilda's elbow and shot Tucker a possessive glare.

"Come along, Mattie," he said. "We've got reservations."

Undaunted, she winked back at Tucker, then allowed her husband to propel her down the street. She patted his arm and said, "I've got no reservations about you, Henry, my always gallant protector."

Tucker shifted so that Lainey could see the departing

couple. Henry raised Matilda's hand and kissed it. Matilda responded with a laugh that made her seem far younger than her years. Then Henry made both Tucker and Lainey laugh when he glanced over his shoulder at them and shot them a quick grin and a wink, before continuing toward the hotel.

"Wily old codger." Lainey smiled with approval at the departing couple.

Tucker tucked her closer to his side. "That's what I want."

"Who wouldn't," she replied with a last wistful glance. When she turned back to him, her expression was sober. "It's not you I don't trust, Tucker. It's me."

"What is it you think you have to do to prove you can trust yourself? How will you ever know you can unless you try?"

Lainey sighed and eased from his grasp. "I want to help Minerva. I want to get that settled." She looked at him, her eyes beseeching him. "For once, I need to follow through on one thing and see it finished before I get involved in the next."

She was mere inches away, yet Tucker felt as if there was an uncrossable chasm in that tiny space. Another kiss could likely bridge the breach, but he knew that conquering her resistance with kisses was a sure way to end up on her list of regrets. It had to be her choice.

"Then let's get Damian out of the way first."

She blinked, obviously surprised by his easy acquiescence.

"Don't get me wrong, Lainey. You can put up as many walls as you like. I will scale them as fast as you build them."

She lifted her chin. "Pretty bold words."

"I have pretty bold feelings where you're concerned." Her expression faltered once more, and he reached out and stroked her cheek again. "We'll go at your pace, Lainey. But we will go."

NINE

Lainey protested his self-assured mandate immediately, mostly because just hearing the certain promise in his words gave her a deep-down, private thrill that felt so wonderfully right, she knew it had to be wrong. "I'm not going anywhere unless I—"

"Do you know if Damian gave Minerva a prospectus of any kind?" he interrupted.

Surprised by the question, she answered automatically. "Yes, I think so, but—"

"Where would it be? Can you get it?"

Lainey frowned at his continued bullying tactics. He'd certainly switched gears easily enough. "I suppose so." She tried not to pout. After all, he was giving her the space she'd asked for, wasn't he? She refused to admit even to herself that she was already regretting yet another decision. But that didn't stop her from wishing she could trade this polite, businesslike Tucker for the hot and barely-in-control Tucker who had whispered dark promises then kissed her in a way that made her believe he could keep them. She swallowed against a suddenly dry throat—the only thing dry about her at the moment—and twisted her fingers together to keep herself from reaching for him and to hell with decisions, rash or otherwise.

"Whatever Damian gave her is probably in her apartment. She lives over the café." Lainey stifled a sigh and forced her mind to the business at hand. "She's out with Lillian and some of the other ladies tonight playing bingo at the community center. They don't usually get home till eleven or twelve."

"Perfect. Let's go." He didn't wait but headed toward the main street.

Lainey trotted after him. "Wait a minute. Let's go where?"

"Minerva's. I assume you have a key, right? Why don't we go take a peek."

"Tucker, I don't know . . ."

He stopped, causing her to almost trip out of her high heels when she banged into him. He steadied her with a firm hand that made her knees wobble for reasons that had nothing to do with her shoes.

I want you, Lainey. She couldn't seem to look at him and not hear those words. *I want you.*

"Do you want to help her or not?"

"Ah . . . of course I want to help her," she said, sounding more breathless than she should. She made herself straighten away from him and smoothed her dress. "I'm just a little uncomfortable about snooping through her things."

"But you'll do it?"

She frowned at him, wondering how in the hell one man could simultaneously make her hair-pulling crazy and so sexually frustrated, she could barely walk straight.

"I don't see where I'm having a real choice here. But what else is new?" She started up the street without waiting for him to follow. "Why I'm trying so hard to make calm, rational decisions around you, I have no idea. Doesn't seem to make any difference, you've got me doing things your way no matter what."

Tucker's deep chuckle came from directly behind her shoulder. "And I'm telling you your judgment is and always has been fine. You're just proving me right."

Lainey ignored him and continued on around the corner, making it to the next one before speaking again. "All the other shops will be closed by now, but I think it might be a good idea to use the alley entrance."

"Good decision."

She shot him a hard look. "Don't push it."

He gave her a "Who me?" look, but it changed to a unrepentant grin under her continuing glare. He shrugged. "Just making an observation."

"Let's get this over with." She let them into the kitchen area of the darkened café, then unlocked another door that opened onto a narrow staircase. "It's up here."

She could feel Tucker's big, warm presence behind her as she climbed the stairs. Her mind tortured her with images of what it would feel like to stop, turn around, and let him step up against her . . . press her against the wall . . . search for her mouth in the dark . . . find it, tease it with soft kisses. . . . She'd sigh and open for him . . . let her hands trail up his sides and over his back . . . grip his shoulders as he took the kiss deeper. . . .

She dropped her keys. "Oh." She was almost panting at this point and didn't trust her knees enough to bend down and fumble around.

"I've got them." His voice was a deep whisper, and it

was close. Oh, so close. She heard the keys jingle. "Lainey?"

"Yes," she said breathlessly, feeling her body sway ever so slightly toward him. She felt the warmth of his body, his breath lightly caressing her cheek as he crowded her on the landing between the top step and the door to Minerva's apartment.

"The keys? You want to unlock the door?"

"Huh?" It took another second for his words to register. Thank goodness it was dark. Her cheeks were on fire—as was the rest of her body. "The keys, right."

"They're right here."

She heard the jingle as he dangled the keys in front of her. She snatched them from his hand, turned, and jabbed the key into the lock. She was a fickle fruitcake, she told herself as she continued to jab at the lock. She wasn't one step closer to being the cool, calm, levelheaded woman she wanted to be. One second she was yelling at Tucker to leave her alone and the next she was ready to jump his bones in a dark stairwell. A dark stairwell leading to her aunt's apartment no less! Maybe her self-improvement plan was doomed to fail. Maybe she would never be able to change.

Maybe she should throw Tucker up against the nearest wall and beg him to take her, and to hell with self-improvement.

"Where's the light switch?"

"Maybe you should get a grip on yourself and do things the way you said you would," she muttered.

"What was that?" he asked distractedly.

She heard him groping the wall next to the door. With a disgusted sigh she reached out and flipped the switch, casting the small apartment in the soft glow of an antique stained-glass foyer lamp. "She keeps her papers in here." Lainey didn't look at Tucker as she stepped past him into the small living room. She was feeling like a consummate fool as well as a sneak, and she wanted this evening to be over as soon as possible.

The sitting room, as her aunt was fond of calling it, was small. Two walls were lined with bookcases, crammed full with well-read books, framed photographs, and a tea-cup collection. A thinly padded floral brocade settee, fronted by a small Queen Anne coffee table and framed with matching end tables, faced the lace-curtained picture window. In contrast there was an overstuffed side chair with a standing lamp in the opposite corner. Lainey stepped unerringly around the faded brocade ottoman placed in front of the chair, reached under the fringed edge of the lampshade, and pulled the chain. This light was a bit brighter, revealing the large knitting basket wedged between the lamp and the chair and the numerous yellowed paperbacks stacked on the small table that ringed the lamp stand.

She knelt in front of the antique oak secretary that occupied the remaining space and reached underneath the bottom drawer. Taped there was a small jeweler's envelope containing a key, which she took out. She opened the desktop and lowered the writing surface, then pressed a small wooden panel inside the desk, which sprung open to reveal a small drawer. She used the key to unlock it and slid it open.

"Quite the sleuth," Tucker said from behind her shoulder.

She'd been aware of his exact location every second but refused to let herself think about it. Her hands were thankfully steady as she lifted up the wooden lid. "She's an Agatha Christie and Ngaio Marsh fan. She only bought this desk because of the secret compartments."

"A worthwhile reason."

Lainey smiled. "I thought so too." She chanced a glance at him. "This was the only one she revealed to me, though."

He smiled back. "A woman has to have her secrets."

Lainey snapped her attention back to the drawer and lifted out a soft binder that had been folded in half. She opened it and scanned the cover. " 'Greensleigh Knolls, the resort for active seniors,' " she read. "There's quite a bit here and . . ." She slid out another stack of papers that had been folded and wedged in the back. She unfolded them, then looked at Tucker. "It looks like a contract."

"Uh-oh."

Lainey's expression must have revealed her thoughts. Tucker took the papers from her hand. "We'll go over this stuff with a fine-tooth comb. I'm sure we'll find a way to prove this is a scam."

"What if it's too late? If she signed this—"

"We'll get her out of it somehow."

"Well, we'll never get all of this read before she gets home. I don't have any idea when she'd check on these papers again, but I don't think we should keep them."

"Lillian has a copier in her office at the salon. I've got the keys. We'll pop over, make copies, and have the originals all back, safe and sound, before Minerva gets home."

Lainey shook her head. "Am I the only one who thinks this is starting to feel like a bad B movie?"

Tucker grinned. "Bad B movies have at least one good thing going for them, though." He headed for the door. "Are you coming with me or do you want to stay here?"

The evening's back on track, she schooled herself. "I'm coming."

He held the door for her. "You're not going to ask me?" he said, as she stepped into the darkness at the top of the stairs.

The light from the foyer caught the irrepressible twinkle in his eyes.

She sighed. "I'm sure it's another bad decision on my part, but what's one more? Okay, what's the best part about bad B movies?"

Tucker pulled the door closed, shutting out all the light, and stepped next to her, crowding her in the small space. His voice was a whisper in the dark. "Because the hero always gets the girl."

"I'm not 'the girl,'" she said, proud of her steady voice. However, her knees had gone all shaky, and she could barely hear over the thrumming beat of her heart.

"Sure you are." He stepped closer. "If I'm the hero, I choose who the girl is." Her back hit the wall. He braced one hand on the wall above her shoulder and leaned in. "And I most definitely choose you."

She could feel his warm breath. His lips were right there for the taking. All she had to do was reach up and . . . She swallowed against a suddenly parched throat. Where had all the air gone? It was her stairwell fantasy, only it was real and about a hundred times better than she could have imagined.

She reached out and gripped the handrail, then slid out from the narrow space between Tucker and the wall and took a step down before she did something . . . impulsive.

"We'd . . ." She cleared her throat. "We'd better get those copies made." She took another step, holding the railing for all she was worth, more to keep from reaching for Tucker than for balance. "It's getting late."

She heard Tucker step down behind her and ordered her feet to keep going. She was in the storage room with her hand on the back door when she felt him move in close behind her.

"It's later than you think, Lainey."

A shiver of pure pleasure tingled down her spine. *Minerva first*, she ordered herself, *think with your head.*

There were times when being responsible was a real drag.

With a resolute tug, she opened the door and stepped out into the humid night air. A single light on a telephone pole cast the alley with a dull yellow glow. She headed straight toward the back of the salon without another look in Tucker's direction.

Tucker smiled at Lainey's quickly retreating form. It had taken all of his self-control and then some to keep from tossing the papers down the stairs and hauling her up against that wall, wrapping those slender legs around his waist and kissing her until she agreed that all this dancing around was exactly that: a prelude to the inevitable. This was definitely the most excruciatingly protracted foreplay he'd ever experienced.

But Tucker wanted more than a hot romp in a dark stairwell. He wanted hot romps whenever and wherever they chose to have them for the next fifty years. He wanted it all. So he'd let her run. Again. Because when they started romping, he damn sure didn't want anything between them but one-hundred-percent unrepentant, open-ended need.

He watched her tuck her hands tightly across her waist and tap her toe as she impatiently waited for him to catch up. *Oh, I've not only caught up, I'm a whole bunch of steps ahead of you*, he thought. He'd backtrack and follow her lead, but that didn't mean he didn't intend to do whatever it took to nudge her down the path of choice. The one that ended in his arms . . . and in his heart.

He walked the last several feet and didn't stop until he was directly in her personal space. There was enough light to see her eyes widen in reaction to his proximity, then narrow warily. She stepped back. He slid a quick glance over the front of her dress, where her crossed arms had pushed up her breasts—her aroused breasts. He smiled even as the ache grew and tightened inside him, then turned toward the door and fished the keys from his suddenly less roomy pants pocket.

He stepped inside and held the door for her. "This way." He waited for the door to click shut behind her, then led the way down a short, dark hallway. Using another key, he let them into a small office. Instead of flipping on the bright fluorescents overhead, he turned on a small chrome desk lamp.

"Is that a—"

"Lava lamp," Tucker finished, staring at the two-foot-high monstrosity that graced the corner of Lillian's postmodern black acrylic desk.

"It's purple."

Tucker understood her reaction; it mirrored his own the first time he'd seen the violet globs oozing up and down inside the glass lamp. "Her favorite color," he said.

She glanced around the room. "It pains me to say this, but it actually goes with her decor." Lainey smiled when he laughed, then quickly turned to the copier and searched for the power switch.

"It's on the right side, in the back," he said.

She found it as the sudden hum of the machine testified.

"It takes a few minutes to run the warm-up program." There were two semicircular, black patent-leather chairs fronting Lillian's desk. Tucker dragged one close to the other, sat down, and motioned to the empty chair. "Why don't we flip through this while we wait? See what we're dealing with here."

Lainey held her position standing guard over the copier, her spine rigid. "If you don't think Lillian will mind, let's just make two copies, put the originals back, and call it a night. We can both go over them on our own, come up with some ideas, and discuss them later."

Tucker reined in a frustrated sigh. Maybe it *was* time to step back a little, give them both some space. Neither his head nor his heart bought that theory. His body was certainly calling in with a very vocal no vote. But there was no doubt that she had to resolve the situation in her own way. The tough part was admitting that his frustration was actually based more on fear than an overdose of unrequited testosterone-fueled lust—fear that when this was all said and done, no matter how he handled it, she might not choose him.

Why the hell was he torturing himself? Why didn't he just see the problem with Minerva through, kiss Lillian good-bye, and take the next plane back to Seattle, where there were probably dozens of women who wouldn't fight off his attentions?

Because, his little voice responded matter-of-factly, there was only one woman's attention he wanted and she was not in Seattle. No, he thought grumpily, she's two feet in front of me, but at least a million miles out of my reach. And his little voice was right. Nothing and no one could have made him get up and leave.

Falling in love was hell.

"Two copies. Okay," he said evenly.

She eyed him warily. "Okay? Just okay?"

Tucker fought not to crush the papers in his hands. "Meaning 'Okay, I'm willing to do this your way,' " he said slowly through clenched teeth as his control eroded. "But only because if I do it the way *I* want to, I risk watching you run away again. And the only direction I want you running in right now is toward me. So, *okay*, we do this your way, slow and easy." His gaze wandered down her body and back up again. He had to lock his knees together when he saw her nipples pressing hard against the soft cotton of her dress. His voice when he spoke again was barely more than a growl. "Because my way would be hard and fast and forever. And I don't think you're ready for that last part. Yet."

She reached behind her blindly and clutched the copier machine for support. He watched with rapt fascination when her throat worked once then again, and almost lost it completely when he looked back at her face and found her staring at his very obvious reaction to her reaction.

He made no attempt to shift, though he would have given anything to rip his pants off all together and assuage the ache that was now bordering on physical pain. "You do that to me with a smile, Lainey." There was no mistaking that she understood what "that" was. "Hell, you don't even have to be in the room. Thinking about your smile does that to me."

She dragged her gaze to his, a beautiful flush darkening her skin. "Tucker—"

"But making me hard isn't what this is all about," he

continued forcefully. "If we're talking stimulation, then I wish we were built so that you could see what you do to my mind. You want to talk aroused, Lainey? You want to talk hot, hungry, and out of control? You should be inside my head right now. Because it's what's up here"—he tapped his forehead—"that makes what's down there so damn intense, I can barely sit still."

She released a rough sigh, then dragged in an audible breath. "So . . . I'm supposed to want you for your mind, is that it, Tucker?"

"I want you to want me with yours," he responded. He nodded at her dress. "I can see that you want me with your body." She stiffened but didn't look away or move. He silently applauded her. "At any other time in my life that would have been enough. Hell, more than enough."

"But not now." She made it a statement.

He shook his head. "Now I want more. And that means waiting for you to figure out what you want and why you want it. You have to be sure, because I'm damn well not going to be added to that stupid list of yours."

"You're angry."

He shook his head, striving to maintain what little patience he had left, with himself more than her. "Impatient is more like it. If I want something, I figure out how to get it and go after it. It's what made my business so successful."

"I'm not a business acquisition."

"I'm well aware of that. But this is new to me, too, Lainey. I sold my business because I wanted a new life, one that wasn't strictly business. But the only handbook I have is the one that got me here in the first place. I don't know how to do things differently. But I'm trying."

She lifted an eyebrow.

He bit off a sigh, then smiled sheepishly. "I said I was trying. Actual achieving it will apparently take a bit longer."

Her smile was brief. She opened her mouth to speak, then apparently changed her mind and shut it again.

"What?" he asked. When she didn't respond, he prodded. "Tell me."

She watched him silently for a moment, then shrugged lightly. "How can you be so sure?" She folded her hands loosely in front of her, twining and untwining her fingers. "Of what you feel, I mean. What if you're making a mistake?"

She was quite serious, and he took a moment before replying. "I'm not sure I can explain the first part. Instinct? I know I want you, and I know I'm feeling something I've never felt before. It's exciting and frustrating and more powerful than any emotion I've had for anyone."

She dipped her chin in a half nod. "Go on." The words were little more than a rough plea, and he pushed on before she decided she didn't want to hear his answer after all.

"My instinct says go after it, don't let something this unique slip away without doing everything you can to explore it. I follow that instinct because I trust it. I mean, you have to trust yourself that way or what else do you have?"

"Now you understand my dilemma," she said softly.

He knew exactly what she meant, but he didn't agree. "That's because you're too caught up in the second part. The part about making mistakes. No one leads a perfect life filled with perfect decisions. It doesn't mean you stop pursuing what you think is important, even if you have nothing more to base that decision on than that it felt right at the moment."

"And if you get hurt? What, you shrug it off?" She straightened away from the copier. "You say the feelings you have for me are totally new. You can't rely on past experience then, so what do you have left? Instincts telling you to go for it. And you trust them. Why? Because you do have the past experience of knowing that the things you've wanted, or felt strongly about, have proven to be worthy of pursuit. So your instinct is nurtured." She folded her arms again. "It's easy to sit there and say you shouldn't let the fear of making mistakes rule your decisions when you don't make many mistakes."

"I make mistakes."

She shook her head. "In business maybe. That's not the kind I'm talking about." She pressed her hand to her chest. "The kind where your heart is involved."

"How can you be so sure my heart wasn't involved?"

"Because you would have had these 'unique' feelings before if that were the case."

She had him there. She'd also punched another large hole in his defenses. He didn't like thinking she'd had those "unique" feelings for someone other than him. Someone who hadn't been worthy of that gift, someone who had hurt her.

"The reason you trust your instincts is because they've led you to make choices with positive outcomes," she went on. "What happens when you listen and follow, and time after time you discover you've made the wrong decision?" She leaned back against the machine again, wrapping her arms around her waist, this time as more of a protective shield than an offensive tactic. "What are you supposed to trust then, Tucker? How do you separate your instinct from your heart?"

He stood, unable to sit there and watch the pain etched on her features and hear the confusion vibrating in her voice.

She held out a hand, stopping him from coming closer. "Answer me."

He stilled, curling his fingers into tight fists against the need to pull her into an embrace and promise her everything would be okay. But he couldn't make that promise. Her problem was serious and one she had to resolve herself. There was no solution, simple or otherwise, he could offer her. He'd never felt so completely helpless. "I don't have the answer." The admission was difficult. He felt as if he was letting her down when she needed him most. What in hell was he supposed to do?

"Then I guess you're going to have to let me find them on my own," she said softly, clearly never expecting it to be otherwise.

"I hate this, Lainey. You're hurt and confused, and it's the very last way I want you to feel around me. I wish it were as simple as saying trust yourself one more time. I wish it were as simple as saying trust me to know that this time it will be okay. But then none of this has been simple, and there are no guarantees."

"Did you ever stop to think you only have feelings for me because I'm the first woman under the age of seventy you've laid eyes on since your big life-changing decision?"

"Not once."

"See? I will never understand that. I question everything. Or at least I'm trying to. I don't always know the right questions to ask myself, but I'm learning."

"Why, Lainey? Why are you trying so hard to be something you're not?" He stepped closer. "Are you really so miserable? Have the mistakes so outweighed the positive choices?"

"Yes." There was no hesitation in her answer, and the pain shadowing her eyes put to rest any lingering doubts he might have had.

What did a man say to that? "Do you have any idea what it is costing me to stand here and watch you in pain and not do something about it?" he said roughly.

Her arms tightened further around her waist and her eyes seemed bigger and more vulnerable than ever. Her voice was a shaky whisper. "Do you have any idea what it is costing me not to say the hell with it and take whatever you have to offer and hope I'll survive another rash decision after you're gone?"

His control snapped. He closed the remaining distance and took hold of her elbows, tugging her arms away from her body, then closing that space as well. She stood rigidly, staring at the center of his chest. "Look at me," he commanded softly. Slowly she raised her head, tilting it back until he could see her teary eyes. His throat tightened and his gut felt like a knot of burning fire. "I'm not going anywhere. Not without you."

"Maybe that's what scares me the most."

"What? I won't ask you to leave here, Lainey, or to leave Minerva. I don't have to go back to Seattle."

"That's not . . ." She stopped and took a second. "If we start this and it doesn't . . . go anywhere, if I can't make it work right and you—"

"Hey, who said it was all up to you to make this relationship work?"

"I'm the one who hasn't been able to pull one off

before, so it stands to reason I'll be the one to somehow screw this up. But you won't give up . . . or maybe that's what I couldn't stand . . . that you would give up, that at some point you'd decide this was really a whim and I'm not what you wanted. I couldn't stand that. Not this time. Not with you."

He cupped her cheek with his hand, his heart beating faster at her soft gasp of response to his touch. "Did it ever occur to you that you wouldn't be so scared if your feelings for me weren't so strong? That being scared is actually a pretty good indication of how important pursuing this is?" He wove his fingers into her hair and tilted her head back. "Lainey, how can you walk away? Of all the things in the world, isn't this exactly the sort of risk that's worth taking?"

"Risk," she said shakily. "There's that word again."

"There are no sure bets." His patience eroded down to its last thread. "We could fall madly in love and I could walk out the door one morning and get hit by a truck. Do we not go for what we can have because of the fear that it might get taken away? What kind of life is that?"

"A safe one."

"Is that what you really want?" He leaned closer. "Safety? Guaranteed successes only?" His mouth hovered above hers. "Say yes and you're a liar, Lainey Cooper. Everything about you, everything that makes you the woman you are, has to be in there screaming no. You act on emotion, not cool logic, because your emotions aren't cool and logical, they're passionate and impulsive and are mainlined straight from your heart. They're the dominant part of who you are, and I think it's a damn shame that you want to strangle them into submission. I don't want a tame, methodical, controlled

Lainey Cooper. I want you." He gripped her more tightly. "I want passionate, excited, rash Lainey Cooper. The one who thinks with her heart first."

He didn't give her time to react. Letting her think hadn't done either of them any good up to this point. Maybe he should keep her thinking with her heart, until she couldn't listen to anything else.

TEN

Lainey barely had time to register his heated words before his even hotter mouth was on hers. *Yes, oh, yes,* her inner voice cried, with the rest of her body united solidly behind it. There was nothing soft or gentle in this kiss. This wasn't a kiss at all, it was a claiming. And, oh, was he convincing.

He didn't wait for permission, nor as it turned out, did he need to. He kissed her deeply, moving his lips over hers, sliding his tongue into her mouth, tantalizing her, tasting her until she thought she'd go mad if she couldn't reciprocate. He gave up nothing and demanded everything until she was gripping his arms to keep from slithering to the floor, reduced to a puddle of need and desire. And even then, wringing soft moans from her with the lightest touch, his relentless pursuit continued. He pulled her closer, wrapped his arms around her, and leaned his weight more fully against her.

She pulled in huge gulps of air when he broke the kiss, leaving her lips softly swollen, her mouth still wet and filled with the taste of him, but never once did she think to tell him to stop. The only sounds she was capable of were soft moans and whimpers as he sampled her chin, ran his tongue along the side of her neck, nibbled her earlobe, and whispered hot words in her ear.

"Passionate, impulsive, rash," he murmured, his voice raw and raspy, like every nerve ending in her body. "That's how you make me feel, Lainey." He moved back to her mouth and kissed her hard, then pulled her lower lip into his mouth and suckled on it. She quivered against him, and he grunted his approval into her mouth as he took it again. "Not cool," he growled. "Not logical." He took his time and set about claiming her mouth all over again. When they were both breathless, he pulled away and pressed his mouth to her temple, holding her tightly against him.

"When I touch you—" She felt a shudder ripple through him and it affected her like nothing had before. His voice vibrated along her skin, accelerating the pulse that pounded hard beneath his lips. "It's not like anything else. It's not feeding a physical need, though Lord know I have a voracious one where you're concerned."

She swallowed a moan. She didn't want him to stop. The revelation didn't shock her. She'd wanted Tucker since the moment she'd laid eyes on him. But what did stun her was the intensity of her need, and not for simple sexual release—though she doubted her body would ever forgive her if she screwed that part up. He was right. He wasn't claiming only her body, he was out to claim her body, mind, and soul. This wasn't simply hormone-driven lust. She knew what mindless sex felt like.

This wasn't remotely mindless. In fact, it was the total opposite. He engaged her on levels that went well beyond sizzling nerve endings and aching body parts. Every touch branded her somewhere far deeper than her skin.

"I need *you*," he said roughly. "You, Lainey. You alone. What I feel for you changes everything. Every aspect is altered, both physical and emotional; it's profoundly unique with you. Kissing you is different. Your taste excites me because it's sweet and hot but mostly because it's yours and yours alone. Touching you . . . feeling your hands on me . . . it's like an electrical current that only operates from one energy source—you. I can't explain it." He broke off and nuzzled her hair, then dipped down and dropped a light kiss on the side of her neck. "I can't explain it," he repeated hoarsely.

"You don't have to." Her voice was raw, needy, but she didn't stop to clear her throat. It was too tight, anyway. "I feel it, too, Tucker."

He tugged her closer still, until she could feel his heart beating against hers. "Have you . . . is this . . ." There was a pause, then she felt him take in a halting breath and release it in a warm, shuddering gust against the sensitive skin beneath her ear. "Have you felt this way before, Lainey?"

His uncertainty touched her the way no aggressive demand ever could have. It made her realize that he was every bit as vulnerable in this situation as she was. She wasn't the only one risking hurt and pain. Her skin flushed more deeply, but this time with shame. She'd been so wrapped up in her past mistakes that all she'd seen was his bold confidence in daring to trust his instincts. It hadn't occurred to her that having confidence didn't lessen the risk or the severity of the potential pain.

"No, I never have," she answered him with complete honesty. "No, I've never felt anything like this."

He lifted his head, making no attempt to shield the relief in his eyes. Her reaction was instant and uncalculated. She smiled. The compelling combination of assuredness and vulnerability was irresistible. Warmth and affection and something that felt too big and dangerous to think about suffused her, and it all poured out into her smile.

He searched her face, not smiling in return. It was that continued wariness—something she so closely identified with—that, more than anything else, began to tear down the strongest of the walls she'd so diligently tried to build around her heart.

"Give us a chance, Lainey. We'll take it slow and easy."

She laughed, feeling suddenly more lighthearted and carefree than she had in . . . she couldn't remember.

"What?" he asked sincerely.

The heady rush of a decision made, a new path to be followed, filled her, and she impulsively wrapped her arms around his waist and tugged his hips to hers. She moaned instinctively as he pressed fully against her. "Well, that just proves my point."

Heat flared in his eyes, and she had to stifle another gasp of pleasure when he refused to let her loosen her grip. All wariness was gone. The confident predator had returned. "Your point being?"

She thrilled to the low rumble of his voice, the promise that threaded through it. There was no doubt he understood her point and then some, but she humored him, anyway. "That no matter how hard we try to behave otherwise, there is nothing slow and easy about either of us."

He smiled now too. His smile was broad and gleaming, and it invited her to share the pleasure that had inspired it. She felt the tension drain from him, which strangely served to heighten the intensity. "I don't suppose there is," he agreed. "But I could tell you that I'll walk out of here right now, agree to let you call the shots, set the pace, because I'm satisfied with the fact that you're giving us a chance. I could tell you that, and it would be the truth."

"You could tell me that . . . but is that what you want to do?"

He held her gaze intently and slowly shook his head. "I want to seduce that mouth of yours again. I want to start on your lips and work my way down until I've tasted all of you. I want to torture both of us by slowly peeling away that dress you're wearing to find what's underneath . . . then peel that away as well. I want to use my mouth, my tongue, my teeth, my hands, my fingertips to explore every inch of you." He brought his mouth within a breath of hers. "And then I want to start all over again . . . and again . . . and again . . . until we're both ready to scream. Then and only then do I want to enter you, push deep inside of you, until there is no part of me that hasn't touched every part of you." His breath was hot and rapid. "That's what I want to do, Lainey. Right now. And tomorrow. And every moment of every day for as long as you'll let me. But you call the shots."

Call the shots? Lainey could barely think coherently. "I, uh . . . We . . ." She tried to clear her throat, but her heart was firmly lodged in it. No one had ever seduced her so thoroughly or made her feel so wanted—and he'd yet to do more than kiss her. The pictures his words painted, the pleasure they promised, the security she felt in his arms . . .

"Your pace," he said. He pressed a kiss on her cheek that was all the more erotic for its sweet lightness. "Your decision."

"No pressure or anything," she managed, her wry intent lost on a soft moan as he pressed another gentle kiss to the side of her chin.

"None," he promised. "Unless you consider this"—he kissed her chin, the tip of her nose, then each eyebrow—"pressure."

"No, no." She barely formed the words. "Not at all. Don't . . . stop on my account." He kissed her temple, then slid his hands into her hair and tilted her head back so that he could reach the base of her throat. "Please don't stop." Her breathing was little more than shallow pants for air. "I'll let you know what I decide in—" She stopped on a sudden inhalation as his mouth dipped to the neckline of her dress and his thumbs reached up to brush ever-so-lightly across her tightly beaded nipples. "A couple of hours," she said with a sigh.

"Hours," he said, dipping his head in agreement. "Hours is good."

"In . . . in the meantime," she said, lifting her head as she drew in another breath, "why don't you take that big, heavy shirt off while I do something about this dress."

Tucker chuckled, and Lainey thought she wouldn't need to take her clothes off; if he got her any hotter, they would melt.

"I think I said something about slow, torturous peeling." He started to crouch, dragging his mouth down over the front of her dress.

Lainey clutched the copier for support. "Slow, peeling, torturous." She gasped. "Yes, I believe you did. Oh,

God . . ." His mouth closed over one nipple, and she almost climaxed right then, the pleasure so ferociously intense, it was almost painful.

"You have exquisitely sensitive nipples. I can't wait to taste them."

"Me either," she croaked.

He shifted his mouth away and continued his slow journey. It was all she could do not to clutch his head and drag it back up until she could feel the sweet weight of his entire body on hers. As if he'd read her mind, he stood and pulled his white shirt from his dark, pleated trousers.

She helped him.

"This doesn't change anything, you know." She popped buttons while he loosened his belt and unclasped his pants.

"I know."

He stopped what he was doing and cupped her neck, drawing her mouth to his for a quick, hard, hot kiss. He pulled back far enough for her to look him in the eyes. "But when you make your decision about me, about us, I want you to have as much information as possible." He pushed his shirt off his shoulders and let it slide to the floor, then took her hands and placed them with firm deliberation on his beautifully molded chest.

She pressed her fingertips into the smooth, taut skin. His skin was warm, almost hot to the touch, the muscles firm and resilient under her searching fingertips.

"Inform yourself." He flashed her a grin. "Please," he added, then gasped when she gently squeezed his erect nipples.

"Seems I'm not the only one who's exquisitely sensitive," she teased.

"Seems you're not," he ground out as she closed her

lips over one. "Oh . . . my . . . G—" The words ended on a long, growling exhale.

It was thrilling to know she could affect him the way he affected her. She was amazed that the pleasure she derived from running her hands over him, touching him, tasting him was as strong and satisfying as the pleasure she received from his touch.

Lainey knew, in some corner of her mind where she'd shoved what little rational thought she still claimed to have, that she might very well live to regret the aftermath of what she was about to do. But there was no way she'd ever regret the act itself. She'd never forgive herself if she walked away right now. Of course, that was supposing she could walk at all. She might not trust herself to handle things correctly afterward, but she did trust Tucker. He understood what she'd meant when she said this wouldn't change anything. He wouldn't mistake this for something it wasn't. And neither would she.

She slid her hands up over his shoulders and linked them behind his neck. "I never knew education could be so . . . enlightening."

Tucker leaned her back. "Enlightening and—" The copier beeped, startling them both, then the top part of the machine grumbled to life and began to shift, making Lainey yelp and jump forward, almost knocking Tucker off his feet. A blinding flash of light followed as they righted themselves and Lainey turned to glare at the offending mood breaker. Only it hadn't broken the mood. Tucker pulled her back against his warm chest and nuzzled at her ear as he wrapped his arms around her waist. "Let's feed this thing some paper and go be alone for a while."

She knew she shouldn't. She should have taken the

beep as a cosmic signal or something, but it felt too perfect in the circle of his arms. She heard herself laugh softly. "Is this where I'm supposed to say your place or mine?"

His chuckle was wickedly sexy. "Oh, I'm not letting you go. I have the perfect place in mind." He leaned over and scooped up the prospectus papers from where he'd dropped them on Lillian's desk, then reached around Lainey and laid the stack in the feeder tray. He continued to nuzzle her and kept one arm around her waist as he punched the correct buttons and started the process.

Distracted both by the copier's beeping and whirring response and Tucker's lips, Lainey didn't give much thought to where Tucker's "perfect place" was . . . until he scooped her up into his arms, surprising a squeal out of her.

"Put me down before you drop me. This isn't the movies. I'm not one of those wraithlike heroines."

"No," he agreed, as he shouldered her out the door into the hallway and started toward the interior of the salon. "But then I don't have to go that far."

"You're simply too chivalrous," she said, but she was giggling. He didn't carry her as if she were a feather, but neither was he truly struggling. Her ego survived unbruised . . . and the rest of her was unabashedly thrilled by his rather cavemanlike behavior. She broke off suddenly as she realized where he was headed. "You aren't."

"I am." He shifted sideways and turned the knob to the massage room, then kicked the door gently open.

"Tucker—"

"Shh." He toed the door shut and a nightlight flickered on, casting a small glow that left most of the room in heavy shadows. He walked to the linen-draped padded table and put her down, urging her to stretch out. "Don't go anywhere." He walked over to the small wheeled table she recognized as the one that held all the oils and lotions. She heard the click of several switches. There was a sudden low hum, then a soft orange glow emanated from the floor as a small ceramic heater purred warmth into the room. Before she could sit up, he was back by her side.

"Roll over. Onto your stomach."

"Tucker, you don't need—"

"Oh, I need. Badly. Let me, Lainey. If you don't enjoy it, I'll stop."

Oh, she had no doubt she'd be transported, but she was still achy and tingly, with muscles clenching in odd places and an almost agitated need that begged her to do something hot, hard, and fast to assuage it. The very last thing she really wanted to do was stretch out and relax.

With gentle, confident hands he urged her onto her stomach. On a long sigh, as he began to knead her shoulders, she complied.

He slid a folded velvety towel under her head. Something wasn't completely right, she thought dazedly. Oh, yeah. "My dress," she murmured. "Shouldn't you—"

"We'll get there, Lainey." He stepped to the foot of the table and slid her shoes off. She wriggled her toes, then moaned as he took one bare foot in his hand and began to slowly work his fingers along the sole of her foot. Somewhere, somehow, he'd rubbed oil into his palms. They were warm, slick, and incredibly arousing. Who knew relaxing could be so intensely erotic? The agitation she'd felt banked down to a low, constant hum of need. She sank deeply into it, gave herself over to it—

and to the man who'd so perceptively stirred it to life within her.

"Right," she agreed blissfully. "Slow. Torturous. How could I have forgotten?" She groaned as he deeply rubbed first one foot, then the other. "This is too good to be legal."

Tucker chuckled and focused twice as hard on working slowly up to her calves. Touching her this way, forcing restraint, was driving him insane. He was a breath away from simply devouring her. Who's stupid idea was it to go slowly? There was no denying it was exquisite torture.

"You *are* a consenting adult," he said, moving past the backs of her knees.

"I'm a begging-you-please adult." The words were muffled against the towel. She'd gone all languid and drowsy on him, but as his fingertips worked farther up her thighs, he felt the tension thrum back into her muscles until she was almost quivering with it.

He'd never been so close to exploding from merely touching a woman. He was climbing out of his skin, and they were both still mostly dressed. He pushed at the hem of her dress, nudging it higher and higher as he worked his fingers into the backs of her thighs.

"An if-you-stop-now-I'll-kill-you adult."

"Mmm, an assault adult." He slid his fingers along the inside of her thighs. "Maybe we can focus all that . . . aggression." His fingertips brushed silk. She groaned and writhed under his touch. A hot lick of pleasure rushed over him. It took every scrap of control he had to keep from climbing onto the table and burying himself inside her right then and there.

"Who's idea was this, anyway," he grumbled. His tortured tone made her laugh, then groan as the movement caused his fingers to brush over her again. She was hot, and there was no mistaking she was ready for him. Scented oils could not compete with scented Lainey.

As he moved to the side of the table, his hands never left her body. He pushed her dress higher, exposing a hint of pale peach silky panties. He groaned. She writhed. He was dying a slow, scented death. His control began to crumble as he nudged her thighs farther apart and slid his fingers along the inside of the soft elastic.

"Tucker." Her demand was part growl, part mindless need. He understood her perfectly.

He leaned down and kissed the side of her neck, surprising a gasp out of her. She lifted her head and turned to him. He took advantage of her parted lips . . . and her parted legs.

Her response was everything he could have hoped for and then some. She reached up and hooked his neck, pulled him closer, and returned his kiss with a power that left him trembling. Her thighs clamped around his wrist as she moved under him, moaned into him, came for him.

Her climax was raw, unabashed, and pure Lainey. He couldn't stand it a moment longer. He pulled her dress over her head even as she reached for his loosened belt buckle. It wasn't graceful, and they were both panting and half laughing by the time their clothes landed in a heap on the floor.

"Highly unprofessional. You'll never get your massage license now," she said, smiling up at him.

She was propped up on one arm, and he pulled her around so that she was sitting on the side of the table, her legs straddling his. He tucked his hands under her thighs and lifted them to his hips. They both moaned as he brushed against her. "What a damn shame." He leaned over her, pressing her back, pressing against her heat.

Her head dropped back, inviting him to taste fully the breasts he'd only grazed earlier. They were amazingly distracting, and he took his sweet time satisfying his sudden craving.

She gasped as he pulled one beaded nipple deeper into his mouth. "How do you do that?"

"This?" He playfully dragged his tongue across the shallow valley between her breasts. "Or this?" He circled her other nipple with his tongue, then teased it gently between his lips.

He urged her legs to lock behind his hips, then slid a hand beneath her neck and lifted her head until she looked at him. In the space of several silent heartbeats, their smiles faded. He looked deeply into her eyes. "Are you ready for me, Lainey? All of me?" He was asking a far bigger question than the obvious.

Her pupils were huge, her lovely green eyes were drowsily seductive . . . but they held his gaze with a certainty that told him she knew exactly what he was asking. "I guess we're about to find out," she whispered.

It wasn't the assured promise he wanted, but it was honest, and that was far better. He began to press inside of her, delighting in seeing how her eyes changed, flashing green fire. He decided he could easily spend the rest of his life watching her as he made love to her. Her smiles, her laughter, her eyes that promised sleepy seduction one moment, then snapped and crackled with heat the next.

No, he'd never grow tired of loving Lainey Cooper.

He buried in his heart the words that crept right to

the edge of his tongue and buried himself inside her at the same time.

They were half frantic and all wild, and it was over long before he wanted it to be. He remained deep within her after their moans had slowed to deep breathing and their shuddering bodies had relaxed. Tucker held Lainey tightly to him, cupping her head to the curve of his neck as he leaned heavily against the table. "I don't want to let you go," he said, his voice a deep rumble. "But I'm going to end up on the floor if I don't—"

"Climb up here with me," she said, her lips warm and damp against his neck.

Just hearing her voice, he actually began to stir. He felt her smile as his own curved his lips.

"Maybe I should have said climb up here *on* me." Her voice was smoky and rough, and he hardened further.

He chuckled and held her even tighter. "Oh, Lainey, where have you been all my life?"

He felt her tense and regretted, for an instant, his comment. But though his timing might not have been the best, he refused to feel bad for speaking the truth. His life before her was the past, over and done with. But his life ahead was filled with possibilities, and he wanted them all to include Lainey Cooper.

She lifted her head and he shifted to allow her to look at him. He hated what he saw in her eyes, hated more what he knew she was going to say, but he also knew— had known all along—that nothing, not even the powerful connection they'd just shared, would circumvent the inevitable. There was no going around it, but he was determined to get them through it.

"Tucker, you understood what I meant earlier."

"You said this wouldn't change anything. I agreed. It

didn't, for me. I already knew how I felt about you, and I knew that making love with you would deepen it, strengthen it, but not change it."

"But that is a change. It alters the risk."

"For me. It was one I was more than willing to take."

She shifted against him, and he reluctantly let her move and sit up, though he kept her legs around him and continued to hold her.

"Will you expect the same from me?"

He knew what she was asking. "I only expect you to be honest with yourself and with me. As I said, I know how I feel, and I think I've made that pretty clear to you. What you feel is something I can't control. Only you can decide that."

"I don't want to hurt you, Tucker."

His heart tightened painfully, and he fought hard to keep that pain out of his eyes. "I'm hoping you won't."

"But—"

"Shh." He pressed his fingers gently to her lips. "I said 'hoping.' Whatever you decide, be honest with me, Lainey. Even if it hurts. But promise me one thing."

"What?"

He dropped a soft kiss on her lips, then brushed his mouth across her cheek. "Be just as honest with yourself."

ELEVEN

Lainey was closing up the café, her thoughts on Tucker, as they had been every minute since they'd parted two nights before, when someone rapped on the front window.

With one hand pressed to her chest, she unlocked and opened the front door. "You scared me half to death."

Tucker stepped inside and out of the way, while she locked the door once again and closed the blinds on the door and front windows. "You were expecting me, weren't you?"

His expression was unreadable. "Yes, I was. I was lost in thought, I guess." The truth was, she'd been expecting him to pop up sooner. Lainey had had catering obligations that had taken up most of her time during the last forty-eight hours, which was why they'd agreed to meet tonight to go over their plans to help Minerva. But given Tucker's pursuit thus far, not to mention what had occurred two nights earlier, she'd jumped at every sound, certain that when she turned, she'd find Tucker lounging against the nearest wall, tree, or building, grinning confidently, ready with a new plan of attack.

But he hadn't. And now that he *was* there, he wasn't smiling or lounging, much less attacking. It was only then that she realized how much she had been counting on him to make the next move. She'd tried to tell herself that she'd been pleased that he'd apparently decided to give her space and to let *her* make the next move. His even expression and somewhat stiff posture as he slid onto a stool at the counter made it clear that he was doing just that.

She should be thrilled. After their conflagration the other night, they were both stepping back and allowing things to progress coolly and logically. So why was it taking all of her control not to scream at him that there was entirely too much space between them and if he didn't haul his very fine backside off that stool and come sweep her into his arms and kiss her senseless, she might go mad?

She knew why. And that was the reason she carefully kept her back to him as she wiped down the last two tables. "I'm almost finished."

"Take your time."

Take your time, she mimicked silently as she scrubbed viciously at a spot of dried ketchup. She'd rather take him. And that was precisely what he was waiting for her to admit.

She moved to the last table. She'd admitted it to herself already. She'd spent two long sleepless nights searching her soul, examining her past, pondering her future. By daybreak she'd concluded that there was no denying she wanted Tucker Morgan, but that was all she'd concluded. She was still confused. She still felt very strongly that her focus had to be on helping Minerva. She'd never forgive herself if she allowed her relationship with Tucker to take off on a whirlwind of lust and passion that was certain to cloud her mind and very likely her judgment and, in the end, cause her to screw up and make a wrong move or miss a possible solution, leaving her aunt to suffer the consequences.

As the hours had passed with no sight or sound of Tucker, she was ashamed to admit she'd even been tempted to take that risk. But when she looked beyond the situation with Minerva, she realized she still wasn't certain. She was afraid. Afraid to fail. Afraid to jump . . . and fall flat on her face. Again. She was still working at trying to be more responsible and levelheaded, and Tucker made her feel anything but. And to confuse her further, he'd told her not to change, to be who she was, but he hadn't dealt with the results of her being Lainey Cooper.

She did know one thing. Whatever her past foibles had wrought, she was happy there. She loved working at the café with Minerva. There had been discussions of her eventually taking over, allowing Minerva to retire, if Lainey decided it was what she wanted to do. Her soul searching had helped her to make that decision. Which only intensified her feeling of responsibility to make sure that Minerva had something to retire on.

Where did that leave Tucker? He'd said he didn't have to leave. But what would he do if he stayed? She understood money was apparently not an immediate concern of his. There was an incredible freedom in that, and she couldn't believe he wouldn't want to take advantage of it and explore all the possibilities his business success allowed. He couldn't do that if he was tied to her, to her life in Sunset Shores and all that it entailed. Even if he did choose her, how long would it be before he regretted settling so soon? And in a senior retirement village to boot?

"I think it's clean. Unless you're trying to change the color of the Formica."

Lainey started guiltily. He was right behind her. She took a breath and carefully smoothed her expression before turning to him. "Never can be too clean. The health department has more rules than the IRS. Their inspectors are scarier too."

He didn't smile. "I think I have a plan that might get Minerva her investment back."

Lainey sighed, feeling the weight settle even heavier on her heart. She'd read all the papers. It hadn't taken a lawyer to determine that Minerva had invested quite heavily in Damian's property development. "I'm all ears. It looked pretty cut and dried to me. The investors don't see any money until the condos are done and start selling. It all looked quite legit, and she signed the contract and wrote the check. Unless we can prove it's a scam and they never intend to build those condos, I don't see how we can get her money back."

"Why don't you sit down before you fall down?"

She'd have been insulted if she'd had the energy. As it was, he was simply stating the obvious.

"Rough day?"

Even rougher nights, she thought, but didn't say it. She merely nodded and slid into a booth.

"Is there still coffee on?" She started to rise, but he motioned her to stay seated. "I know where it is, remember?"

She detected a hint of his old smile and felt a rush of

relief that was almost embarrassing. *Get a grip, Lainey. Think cool. Logical.* "It's hot and fairly fresh. The mugs are stacked—"

"Got it," he interrupted. She let him. Even when he was obviously playing the business consultant and platonic friend, he didn't make her feel remotely cool or logical. If anything, her confusion factor had doubled.

"I spoke to that investor friend of mine again yesterday," he said as he unlatched the door and stepped behind the counter. "He has some other property he's developing in Miami, close to where this project supposedly is, and he looked into it. The land is there and it is posted for the development, but ground hasn't been broken."

"So it's legitimate?"

He filled two mugs and crossed back to the booth. "On the surface it is. It's a tangle of paperwork, but between us we managed to trace it back through several corporations to a holding company." He slid one mug in front of her and sat down. "Guess where they're headquartered?"

"Here?"

"Bingo. Actually, the offices are in Tampa, but that's close enough. I imagine there's probably another company to which the profits are diverted tucked somewhere nice and tax-free."

She shook her head slowly, then sipped her coffee. "I don't know, Tucker. It still doesn't add up to me. I can't see Damian running something this big, legit or otherwise."

"That's just it, he's not."

"But you said—"

"We're agreed Damian's not stupid, right?" She nodded. "He knows what his strengths are, and you're right, running something this big is beyond his capabilities. However, this is where the money is."

She set her mug down as understanding dawned. "He's a partner, or in a kind of junior executive sort of position."

"Give the lady a prize. Damian marketed his best asset to the big boys—his skill in getting people to give up their money—which he does for a cut of the take."

"Can we prove this? I know if you explained this to Minerva, she'd believe it now." Lainey had decided to hold off telling her aunt anything until she'd had a chance to talk to Tucker, knowing it would be easier if she presented a solution along with the bad news. "But that won't get her money back or Betty Louise's or Bernice's. Will it?"

"First of all, proving it is close to impossible. These guys are slick and they're pros. At this point the thing is legit. It will be several years until they max out their various lease and contract options—and bleed dry as many people as they can in the process—before they fold up shop and disappear into the night."

"Only to set up shop in some new town, with a new phony scam. Hell, if they really own that land, they can probably put up a new sign and run the same scam again and again."

"And you said that business degree was gathering dust."

Lainey felt a shot of warmth all the way to her toes when she looked up to find him smiling at her. And it had nothing to do with his pride in her business accumen. "No, Damian said that. But even if I've put that piece of paper to use helping Minerva reorganize the way she runs this café, it won't help me get her out of this mess."

She watched Tucker's smile fade, his expression still intent . . . almost bemused. Disconcerted, she glanced back at her coffee and took another sip. "So you're saying it would be years, if ever, before we could actually nail these guys."

She glanced up in time to catch him staring at her before he ducked his gaze back to his coffee. She worked to not squirm in her seat. It had barely been a blink of time, but she swore she'd seen a flash of . . . well, the only word she could come up with was hunger. There had been unabashed, unadulterated hunger in his eyes. Maybe it wasn't any easier for him to back off than it was for her.

How long would it be before one or the other's control snapped and they found themselves naked and going at each other on the counter of Minerva's café?

She took a large swallow of coffee and tried not to choke. Who was she kidding? One brief hint of a glance and she was almost ready to crawl across the table into his lap. She was still only playing at being responsible, playing at being cool and levelheaded.

"Even if we went to Roscoe or the feds and they agreed to look into it, yes, it would likely be years."

The low rumble of his voice sent shivers of awareness through her. How long could she keep this up? The answer curled around her heart like a cold fist. She couldn't. She couldn't stay around Tucker and be the person she wanted to be, knew she had to be, to avoid future disasters.

"So what do I do?" She knew he heard the bleak hopelessness in her voice, but only she knew the true depth of her question.

"We," he corrected. "What will we do." He reached

out and covered her hand. She jumped at the zap of electricity the contact sent shooting through her. It took all of her willpower to keep from yanking her hand away.

She wanted to yell that "we" couldn't do anything, because she couldn't handle being a "we" with him. She'd never learn to control her impulses if every time she got the urge to jump, he stood right behind her, willing to push.

But they were dealing with saving Minerva's money right now, and Tucker was the one with the connections to help. She had to push aside what she felt for Tucker in order to focus on Minerva, then carefully explain to him that she couldn't pursue a relationship with him, in a way she hoped he would understand. It was her only hope.

Cool. Logical. Responsible.

Now if she could only summon up enough courage and control and force it past the crushing pain in her chest, so she could look him in the eye and follow through on it.

She took a deep breath and lifted her head, only to find him staring at her. She swallowed hard. There was no banked hunger, at least none that she could see. In fact, she couldn't see anything in his eyes. However, it took all of her persuasive powers to convince herself that he couldn't see exactly what she was thinking, know what she was planning. "You said you had a plan?"

He nodded, his gaze still firmly on hers. She knew he suspected that all was not right inside her scattered head, but he was going to help her, anyway. Of course, Tucker was nothing if not determined. He was backing off, helping her with Minerva the way she'd asked him to, with realistic hopes that afterward she would consent to continue and deepen their relationship.

"It's not exactly kosher," he said, shifting forward, leaning over his coffee mug. "Sort of a take on the old 'if you can't beat 'em, join 'em' routine."

She couldn't do this, couldn't let him help her out when she was planning to dump him right after. She had to tell him now, up front, even if it meant that he walked out of the café and her life forever. It might not be the most responsible way to handle things where Minerva was concerned, but it was the honest way. Even Minerva would understand and approve of that.

"Tucker, listen, there's something I—" Lainey broke off, startled when someone knocked on the front door hard enough to rattle the aluminum miniblinds.

She caught Tucker glancing at his watch. "She's early."

"Who's earl—" The blinds rattled under a renewed assault. Lainey got up and flipped up the blinds. She glanced over at Tucker. "Lillian?"

"I was about to explain."

Confused and more than a little curious, Lainey turned the lock and let the woman into the café. Lillian strolled past her, unsnapped the front of her red silk turban, flung her arms wide, and turned in a small circle.

"Whaddya think?"

Lainey's mouth dropped open. Gone was Lillian's white blond pouf of helmet hair. In its place was a sleekly styled, jet-black cap of elegantly arranged waves, reminiscent of Joan Collins's most famous role, the bitchy Alexis. With exquisitely sculpted pencil-thin eyebrows, subdued makeup that took years off her appearance, a wicked slash of red on her expertly outlined lips, and discreet gold and diamond earrings clasped to her ears, all Lillian needed was a Dior suit and black Italian pumps and she'd be the quintessential grande dame power magnate. As it was, the red silk track suit and high-top white sneakers she was wearing made Lainey a bit dizzy.

Lillian ended her one-woman show facing Lainey, who immediately snapped her mouth shut and scrambled for something to say.

Lillian shot a look at Tucker. "You haven't told her yet, have you?"

Tucker shook his head and got as far as opening his mouth before Lillian sighed dramatically and grabbed Lainey's hand. "Never mind. I'll do the talking." She slid into the booth across from Tucker, then motioned for Lainey to slide in next to her. "What have you two been doing, anyway?" She cast a sharp look at one then the other and paused.

Despite the fact that nothing had been going on, Lainey felt her cheeks heating up as images of what she'd done in Lillian's salon two nights earlier flashed through her mind. She was certain that Lillian could see every damning thought written clearly on her face.

She pulled her hand from Lillian's and scooted out of the booth. "Let me get another mug and the pot of coffee," she said, not giving anyone a chance to refuse. "I have a feeling we're going to need it," she added under her breath.

"Tucker explained to me all about this Damian character," Lillian began.

Lainey grabbed a mug and the pot and headed back to the booth.

"We're going to nail the little weasel," Lillian continued.

If she hadn't been so tied up in knots over Tucker and this whole mess, Lainey would have laughed at the relish in Lillian's voice. She sat down and filled everyone's mugs. " 'We'?" she asked, trying her best not to stare at Lillian's hair.

"I've talked it over with Lillian, and with some help from my investor client-friend, I think we can pull this off."

"Pull what off?" Lainey looked with exasperation and not a little trepidation at the two.

Lillian patted Tucker's hand and smiled. "It's a brilliant plan. It will work." She turned to Lainey. "Tucker's investor is going to provide us with some brochures and contracts and prospectus information on a project he started but scrapped when the landowner died and his heirs decided not to sell. It's for some property here in Florida, near St. Augustine."

A knot of dread coiled in her stomach. Lainey was afraid that she knew exactly where Lillian was headed with this. "You don't mean to set up your own scam, do you?"

"That's exactly what we're going to do," Tucker said. "I have two suites reserved at the Fairmont, and the necessary equipment to set up an office is being delivered there today. Roger—that's my former client—is expressing all the other stuff today. We should be ready to roll by tomorrow."

"Tomorrow?" Lainey said weakly. "But what if Damian recognizes you?"

"I won't be directly involved." He nodded to Lillian.

"Minerva met this guy at the hotel," Lillian went on. "He hasn't been in the salon or ever laid eyes on me. And on the off chance he's ever seen me out with Minerva somewhere, I did the makeover. Besides, he's not interested in anyone else right around here. Tucker says he keeps his groups of investors in any one area to a small minimum to lessen the chance that they can combine forces to track down proof of the scam after it's over. Now, look at this."

Lillian pulled her purse up and dug out a small gold business-card holder. She slipped out a nice vellum business card and flashed it at Lainey, then slid another out for Tucker.

"Great, huh? I had them done at that quickie place over in Hampton this morning." The card was engraved in black, with the name "Lila Parks" centered in elegant script. Under that were the words "International Development and Investments." The hotel's name and number, along with the name of her suite and the extension, were listed discreetly in one corner.

"You didn't need to do this, Aunt Lillian." Tucker smiled at her. "But it is a nice touch."

Lainey was overwhelmed by their preposterous plan, but not enough to miss Tucker's smile and feel a pang of envy mix with the clutch of pain at the thought of never being on the receiving end of one of them again.

Striving for a calm, rational voice, she said, "I think it's wonderful that you're willing to do this, Lillian." She turned to Tucker. "And it's more than generous of you to underwrite the expense."

"Our pleasure," Lillian said, casting another penetrating glance between Tucker and Lainey. "It's the least we can do for a friend, especially one that feels like family."

Lainey didn't miss the underlying meaning, but now was not the time to dissuade Lillian from her matchmaking intentions. That would take care of itself soon enough. "I think that's wonderful. But don't you both think this plan is, well . . ."

"Exciting?" Lillian put in. She patted Lainey's hand. "It's brilliant."

"Complicated," Lainey said, compromising on the terms she'd wanted to use. "Rash," "ridiculous," and "dangerous" all came to mind.

"Nonsense. I set up a meeting with Damian. I plan to get him to agree to come to work for me, doing the same thing he's doing now, which is admitting he's a crook." She pounded the table, making both Tucker and Lainey flinch. "Then we've got him!"

"You're bringing the police into this? Roscoe? Isn't this entrapment or something?"

"No Roscoe," Lillian answered before Tucker could respond. "And only law enforcers can entrap someone."

"No police? I assumed you were trying to get him arrested."

Tucker spoke up. "Arrested doesn't get Minerva's money back."

"Extortion does," Lillian added, her eyes gleaming.

Lainey looked at both of them as if they'd lost their minds. "You're going to blackmail him?"

"Yup. Then, when he brings the money back, we'll arrest him."

Lainey slumped back in her seat. "I can't believe I'm listening to this." She took a deep breath, then sat up straight and braced her hands on the table. "I can't let you do this. It's too dangerous. Too irresponsible."

"And we wouldn't want that, would we, Lainey."

She shot a look at Tucker. His gaze was hooded and unreadable. She was aware of Lillian's avid attention and knew that now was not the time to get into the issue. She sent him a look that told him they weren't done and looked back at Lillian.

"Listen, I think it's wonderful that you want to help. But this is much too extreme a measure to take."

"Tucker said most of Minerva's life's savings were at stake. That's a pretty extreme problem and it calls for pretty extreme measures, don't you think? And what have we got to lose by trying?"

Valuable time, Lainey thought.

"Do you have any better ideas, Lainey?" Tucker asked laconically. "Logical, rational, or otherwise?"

Lillian's sharp, disapproving inhale grabbed their attention. "I don't know what is going on between you two, although I have a pretty good idea. Whatever the problem, I think we need to concentrate on Minerva right now. You can hash this out afterward." Lillian turned and nailed Lainey with a gaze as sharp as her red razor nails. "And when we do take care of this matter—and we will— I expect the two of you to sit down and talk this thing out until you're blue in the face, if that's what it takes." She shot a hard look at Tucker. "And if that doesn't work, I'll loan you those videos again. Use them this time."

Lainey was only saved from complete humiliation by the fact that Tucker's face looked as bright red as hers felt.

"Now scoot on out of here." Lillian motioned to Lainey. "I'd better skedaddle before Minerva gets back from her visit to the home. You two better scoot as well."

Lillian snapped her turban back into place and stepped toward the door. As she passed Lainey, she placed a hand on her shoulder and said, "I wish we had the time to do something a bit more foolproof. We'd all like to have that luxury. But sometimes you just have to go with what you've got. God gave us instincts for a reason."

She was gone before Lainey could reply. Lainey was still staring at the aluminum blinds clinking against the door when she felt Tucker behind her. "You told her, didn't you."

He didn't pretend not to understand. "About us? No. Maybe Minerva has talked about you, or maybe she figured it out on her own by looking at us. There was a bit of tension in the air."

He placed his hands on her shoulders and turned her to face him. She felt a ripple of pleasure shudder through her at his warm touch. She wanted to beg him to never let her go.

"She's right, you know," he said. "About instincts." He tilted her head back until she looked him in the eyes. "They're not always infallible and neither are you. But where we're concerned, they haven't steered you too far wrong, have they, Lainey?"

"Tucker, I—"

He pulled a card from his pocket and handed it to her. It was a Fairmont Hotel business card. "I had Damian contacted at the number we got from your aunt's papers. We're setting up a meeting for tomorrow night at nine. We plan to meet in the suite across the hall an hour before to set everything up. I'd like you to be there. The number is on the back of the card."

She stared at it, then looked at him and nodded. "There's so much going on. You know I appreciate this." She nodded at the card. "But we have to talk. I need to explain—"

He cut her off with a kiss. It was hot, and it was over before she could beat herself up for responding. "Follow your instincts, Lainey. I'm following mine." He stepped around her and was gone.

TWELVE

"So if you're the, uh, how did you put it? Brains behind the brawn?" Damian jerked his head toward the men beside Lillian. "Who are these guys?"

Lillian spared a glance at Sven and Stephan, who flanked the high-backed leather chair she sat in. She pulled herself closer to her desk and waved the long malachite cigarette holder she held gracefully between two sharply manicured red-clawed fingers. "Associates, Mr. Winters."

Damian looked skeptical. He nodded to Sven. "Have we met somewhere before?"

Lillian's smile was polished and smooth but didn't reach her eyes. "Do you follow professional sports?"

"Not really." He glanced back at Sven. "Did you play ball or something?"

"Or something," Lillian answered for him. "Now why don't we get to the business at hand." She took a long drag on her cigarette and leaned back in her chair.

Lainey groaned and rolled her eyes. "She's gone from Alexis to Cruella." She turned to the ladies crowded around the second television monitor. "Bernice, Betty Louise, Aunt Minerva, I'm so sorry. I should never have—"

"Shh," Tucker interrupted. "She's doing great." He turned to the women. "Don't you think so?"

Minerva, Bernice, and Betty Louise all nodded.

"She should have been in the theater," Minerva said.

"A shame Bunny is the director of the local troupe down at the center," put in Betty Louise. "Lillian would be a shoo-in for the lead in our fall production of *Mame*."

"Never could abide that MacAfee woman," Bernice muttered. "Thinks she's Barbra Streisand or something."

"Shh." Tucker quieted them. "Listen. She's going for the kill."

All eyes turned avidly back to the screens. Lainey found hers lingering on Tucker. Though she'd felt his gaze on her many times during the day, he'd been all business. And with the surprise addition of Minerva, Bernice, and Betty Louise, Lainey hadn't had a chance to speak to him alone at all. Not that she was sure any longer what she wanted to say to him.

She turned her attention to the ladies. They all had confidence in Tucker's plan. Even with their life's savings at stake, Lainey knew their appreciation for the trouble Lillian had undertaken to try to help them meant more than getting their money back. Loyalty. True friendship. Tucker offered those most valuable gifts to her. She shifted her gaze back to him and felt her heart thump a bit faster. She thought about what he was doing for the woman he thought of as family. There was no doubt that this was a man who'd do whatever it took, who would stand by those he loved no matter what. He wasn't Conrad; he certainly wasn't Charlie. And he valued the very traits in her that she herself had been afraid to trust.

That's what it all boiled down to: trusting herself.

Lillian's voice jerked her attention back to the screen.

"I trust we've given you all the necessary information to make a decision," Lillian went on. "So, Mr. Winters, do we have a deal?"

Damian shifted in his seat and recrossed his legs. "Well, this is quite an offer you're making me. I have to admit that I'm flattered, but—"

"Nonsense, Mr. Winters. Flattery has nothing to do with it. I needed someone with your, shall we say, excellent social skills. I did my research and you came up as the best candidate. Now that I've had the chance to talk with you, I've made my decision. I've made you a sound offer."

"You never actually said how it was that you heard about me."

"This is a smaller industry than you might think. My contacts are . . . extensive." She leaned forward. "I know what I want and how to go after it. You strike me as someone who understands that philosophy."

Damian smiled as he relaxed and leaned back in his chair. "That I do, Ms. Parks, that I do. Allow me to look over these papers, and I'm sure we can come to some sort of—"

"I'm also someone who has no patience for indecisiveness," she cut in ruthlessly. "I need someone who can make snap judgments. That's what got me here, Mr. Winters. Making important decisions, then moving swiftly while others pondered their options. The kill goes to the swiftest." She glanced over her shoulder. "Don't you agree, gentlemen?"

Stephan and Sven both grunted, neither taking his gaze from Damian, who sat a bit straighter.

Lillian's smile was sharp enough to cut glass. "So, Mr. Winters, do we have a deal or don't we? I don't make an offer twice."

Lainey realized she was holding her breath. *Sign it, sign it*, she repeated silently. Until that moment she hadn't let herself believe that this might actually work. Minerva had taken her aside that morning and issued a tearful thanks for Lainey's perseverance. Lainey had been shocked at how suddenly old and frail Minerva looked to her. She was also shamed by her aunt's obvious relief. It had been Tucker who had pushed and taken the leap of faith when it was necessary. She felt as if she'd let Minerva down and had told her so.

Minerva had waved away the apology and made a point of telling Lainey that it was what motivated decisions that mattered more than the decisions themselves. The important thing was that her friends and family cared enough to want to help her. Damian would be stopped before someone else was duped, and if they were lucky, they'd get their money back as well.

Come on, Damian, she urged silently. Lainey cut a glance toward Tucker, whose attention was riveted to the screen. He was grinning as Lillian played Damian like a fiddle, but Lainey didn't miss the tension in his jaw or the way his hands gripped the arms of the chair. There was no doubt how deeply he cared. For Lillian, Minerva, the ladies. For her. Her own hands tightened their grip, but her anxiety had a different cause.

She turned her attention back to the monitor and watched as Damian eyed Lillian, Sven, and Stephan, then shifted his attention to the gulf, which spread out beyond the panoramic glass windows.

"Do it," she murmured under her breath. "Sign the papers, you greedy little weasel." In the next instant a hand covered hers and squeezed. She turned to find Tucker staring at her. His touch grounded her, centered her. No matter what happened, they were the core of what was important in her life. She was surrounded by people she loved and cared about and who felt the same about her. And that group included Tucker. It made no difference if they took wrong turns or made a bad choice now and then, she loved them no matter what. Just as they all loved her. She loved Tucker that way too.

The certainty of that knowledge filled her with a radiant joy. Yes, she loved this man, and she wanted his special brand of love in return. With an almost fierce possessiveness, she held his hand tightly. "Thank you," she whispered, putting more into those words than he could possibly understand.

There was a collective inhale from the ladies watching the other monitor. Lainey's attention darted back to the screen before Tucker had a chance to reply. Damian had uncrossed his legs and was standing up. Tucker turned her hand over and wove his fingers through hers.

"Okay," Damian said. "You've got yourself a new associate."

A whoop of joy went up in the room. They were in the suite of rooms across the hall and likely couldn't be heard, but there was no use taking chances. Grinning, Tucker hushed the excited talk with a slashing motion across his neck. "Listen." He pointed to the monitor. "It's not completely over yet."

They watched Damian shake Lillian's hand and sign

the bottom of several papers with a flourish. Lillian checked them over, then folded and handed them to Sven, who tucked them in the breast pocket of his expertly tailored suit. She turned a beaming smile to Damian. "Now there's someone I'd like you to meet. You two will be working closely together."

Damian turned as a tall gentleman entered from another room in the suite.

"Mr. Winters, meet another friend of mine, Mr. Frank Halliday. Perhaps you've heard of him. He's the producer for that lovely television program, *Exposé*."

Damian's face went pale, then flushed as he spun around. "Just what in the hell are you trying to pull here, lady?"

Everyone in the room across the hall tensed. This was the tricky part.

"Sit down, Mr. Winters," Lillian said calmly. Sven and Stephan closed ranks beside her as Damian continued to stand. She motioned Halliday closer. "Your first assignment will be to retrieve from your former employer a specific sum of money and return it to me."

Confused but more belligerent than nervous, Damian scowled. "You're crazy. I'm not stealing from Mr. Fontana. Not for you or anyone."

"While loyalty is an admirable quality, Mr. Winters, I think you'll find that in this case the trait won't hold its usual priority."

"I don't give a rat's behind about loyalty," Damian said.

Lainey tensed as she heard the civilized veneer slip from Damian's voice. This was the man who'd threatened her on the street. Tucker had assured her that no one would get hurt, but she'd had those fierce black eyes leveled on hers, she'd seen the cold indifference change to heated rage.

"If I steal from Fontana, I'm dead. It's that simple."

"If you don't obtain this money for me, then you will wish you were, Mr. Winters." Lillian puffed on her cigarette. "It's that simple."

Bernice gave a low whistle, and Betty Louise wrung another twist in her hanky.

"Go get 'em, Lil," said Minerva.

"She is amazing," Lainey murmured.

"That she is," Tucker agreed. But his smile had a nervous edge. "Come on, Lillian," he urged the screen. "Finish it up."

Damian apparently didn't doubt Lillian's threat. He raked his hand through his hair and began to pace in front of her desk. "You didn't hire me for my people skills, you conned me into signing that contract because you want to bring down Fontana's organization. Who the hell are you, anyway?"

"You don't need to know that," Lillian said with the perfect amount of disinterest. "What you do need to know is that if you don't cooperate with Mr. Halliday and myself, you will be facing a very certain and very long prison sentence. An attractive man such as you might find that environment a bit, well . . . taxing."

"What does the money have to do with it? If all you want is tabloid TV, then—"

"The money is personal. Let's just say Fontana owes me. He stole from certain friends of mine. I want that money back before I bring him down."

"And what guarantee do I have that if I help you, I won't go down, anyway?"

Lillian's grin would have made Cruella herself envious. "You'll have to trust me."

Damian stopped short in front of Lillian's desk. "The hell I will," he said with a growl. He slid his hand inside his jacket pocket and pulled out a nice, neat black revolver. "I'd rather trust this."

The ladies gasped. Betty Louise stifled a shriek with her hanky, as Lillian's eyes widened in obvious surprise.

"Son of a bitch." Tucker shot to his feet, but Lainey was faster.

"Don't." She blocked his path to the door.

Tucker stopped right in front of her, his eyes blazing. "In case you didn't happen to notice, your old college friend in there has a gun."

"I see that, Tucker, and I'm as scared to death for Lillian as you are. I've looked Damian in the eyes and I know he's capable of seeming pretty cold-blooded."

"Then why the hell won't you move so I can do something?"

"I said 'seeming.' We all agreed that in looking at his history, he's never been known to be violent."

"He's never been nailed before, either. It can make a man do desperate things."

"We all also agreed that he's not stupid. Too greedy to always be smart, or he wouldn't have signed that contract, but he's not stupid enough to shoot someone in cold blood, Tucker. Much less four someones. He's outnumbered."

"His bullets even things up. I can't take that chance, Lainey." He tried to push past her.

"What will rushing in there do?" Lainey grabbed his arm. She motioned to the monitor. "Look. Lillian is calm, she's talking to him. He's listening."

"He's still pointing a gun at her." Tucker's jaw was clenched so tightly, it made the vein in his temple jump.

"Exactly. And any kind of sudden move could make him panic. There are four people in there, Tucker. He's not going to go from being a two-bit crook to a multiple murderer. I know he won't shoot. I *know* it."

Tucker speared her with a hard look. "How can you be so damn sure?"

She held his gaze. "Instincts."

Tucker choked on a half laugh. "You pick *now* to put them to a test?"

She ignored that deserved barb. He was scared and angry, at Damian and at himself. "Trust your instincts, too, Tucker. You believed she could do this or you wouldn't have gone to all this trouble. Give the four people in that room a chance to work this out."

"Come here, come here," Minerva said excitedly. "Mr. Halliday is talking to him now!"

Tucker stared at the door, then back at Lainey. She tensed. The stakes were the highest they'd ever been in her life. She didn't back down. "Isn't this what you wanted?" she queried softly. "For me to trust myself? I trust you, Tucker. It's why I'm here. I believe you trusted me too. Have I made another bad decision in believing in you?"

"Lainey, there's more at stake here than—"

She stepped aside and motioned to the door. "Then follow your instincts."

Tucker heard the words he'd tossed so cavalierly in her face the night before thrown down like a gauntlet between them. He stared long and hard at her. She held his gaze unwaveringly. He had no idea what had happened in the last twenty-four hours to finally make her see the light, but . . .

He turned back to the room. "Okay. But if he so much as—"

Lainey glanced at the monitor. "He put the gun down, Tucker." She turned back to him. "He put the gun down! I was right!" She wrapped her arms around him in a bear hug as the ladies cheered. "I did it," she whispered. "I was right."

"You pick a hell of a way to prove a point," he said, holding her just as tightly.

"It's one of my more lovable traits," she said dryly.

Her eyes popped wide when he grabbed her head and pulled her close for a hard, fast kiss. "I've been meaning to talk to you about that."

"About what?" she said in dazed confusion when he released her.

"Being lovable." He pulled her hand. "I'll tell you just how much after this is over."

"Stop dancing around the doorway, you two, and get back over here," Bernice said. "It looks like he's going to do it."

Tucker pulled her back for one more kiss. "I do love you, Lainey."

"I finally got it right." She smiled up at him. "I love you, Tucker. Thank you for believing in me. For showing me how to believe in myself."

"Always have, always will. I won't let you down, Lainey."

"I know. I truly know."

"Did you really say you love me?" She nodded, and he rubbed his chest. "I think my heart is about to explode."

He shot her a grin. "Come on, let's watch Lillian finish doing her number on this weasel. Then I'll kill him."

She sighed and pressed a hand to her heart. "You say the most romantic things."

He winked and pulled her with him back into the room. "And just think, this is only the beginning."

Lainey pulled their joined hands up and pressed a kiss to his fingers. Her eyes shining, she said, "I can hardly wait."

EPILOGUE

In the end it had taken a weasel to trick a weasel. Damian could take lessons on snake-oil salesmanship from Frank Halliday. He had managed to persuade Damian to put away his gun by explaining that everything Damian was doing was being filmed on a hidden camera that could send the transmission to the local police headquarters at the flip of a modem switch. The last part was a small fib, but Damian was already on the hook.

Halliday went on to explain that if Damian could come up with the dirt for Halliday's exposé of Fontana, he would be eligible for a hefty finder's fee from Halliday's television network. He named a figure that made everyone's eyes pop wide except for Lillian's. She smoothly interjected that if Damian surrendered a certain share of that figure to her and destroyed all the copies of the contracts that he'd made while in Florida, she would tear up his contract with her. To everyone's amazement and immense relief, he agreed.

The whole thing had taken thirty minutes. It had taken less than half of that for the word to get around about Tucker and Lainey. Damian and Halliday hadn't even left the building before the ladies had already begun planning the wedding.

Lainey paced in Lillian's office a week later, waiting for Tucker and Lillian to get back. They'd gone this morning to meet with Damian and Halliday to retrieve the money and the contracts. If all went well, Halliday would take over working with Damian on the Fontana story and they'd be out of the picture for good.

They were thirty minutes late.

Just then the door burst open and Lillian strolled into the room. Her new look had been an instant hit with the salon's clientele, so she'd opted to keep it. She had her hair up in a tight twist with two black chopsticks stuck into it. Lainey had to admit that it did go with her mandarin-style top. Which was a startling shade of crimson. Lillian waved a package at Lainey, flashing matching red nails with Oriental characters neatly painted on them.

"We did it," she crowed. "The little weasel came up with the goods!" She hugged Lainey, who was certain she heard her ribs crack, then turned to the door. "Well, don't stand around out there."

Lainey turned to find Tucker lounging in the doorway. "I didn't want to risk another hug," he said, rubbing his sides.

He turned his gaze to Lainey. "Sorry we took so long. I stopped at the executive offices at the Fairmont to talk with management about some consulting work. I showed them a carefully edited clip of our tape of Damian waving a gun at a hotel guest, and they agreed they might need to rethink some of their security measures." He let a slow smile slide across his face. "Did you worry about me?"

Lainey wanted to hug herself as she basked in the

warmth of his gaze. "Not in the least. You had Lillian there to watch out for you."

"That's my girl," Lillian said. She glanced at her wrist. "We got back just in time too."

Lainey forced her gaze away from her future husband and turned around. "Time for what?" she asked warily.

"Your bridal shower."

"My bridal—" She broke off and looked at Tucker. "Did you know anything about this?"

"Who, me?"

She narrowed her gaze, but there was a smile flickering at the corners of her mouth. "You could have warned me."

He held his arms out. "Hey, they threatened to have a bachelor party for me if I ratted."

She flashed a look of mock horror. "Well, in that case you're forgiven."

"I thought you'd understand."

"Enough standing around." Lillian bustled past her to the door. "I have to run next door and give this to Minerva."

Lainey stopped her with a hand on her shoulder. "Lillian, I don't know if I thanked you for all that you've done. I—"

"Nonsense," Lillian said. "Just take care of this one here"—she nodded at a grinning Tucker—"and we'll call it even."

Lainey smiled. "My pleasure."

Tucker stepped into the room and pulled Lainey back against him. "I've been meaning to speak to you about that."

Lillian went out and closed the door, then stuck her head back inside. "You've got fifteen minutes, then I'm coming back to get you. Don't do or say anything to make her mad, Tucker, the whole gang is next door waiting. They've spent all morning getting the place ready." She started to close the door, then opened it again. "Oh, yes, Irma and Ida asked me if they could go with us later today to look at dresses."

"Dresses?" Lainey looked at Tucker, who shrugged. She looked at Lillian. "What dresses?"

"Didn't Minerva tell you? We made an appointment at Betty Louise's Bridal Boutique for three-thirty."

"But I, that is, we—"

Tucker leaned down and whispered in her ear. "I don't care what you wear to marry me, Lainey, as long as you marry me."

She melted against him. "Fine," she said weakly. "Three-thirty sounds fine."

Lillian winked at Tucker. "Remember, fifteen minutes. And stay out of the massage room. Stephan is particular about who touches his oil bottles." She shut the door on a flushing Lainey and a chuckling Tucker.

He pulled her up tight. "And to think I thought the jet set had all the fun."

She looked up at him. "Are you sure you're ready for all of this?"

He nodded without a second's hesitation. "You know you don't have to go with them. I can talk to Lillian."

She shook her head. "No, they're as excited about this as we are. I won't spoil their fun. You just have to promise not to laugh when I come down the aisle."

"Is Lillian going on this shopping trip?"

"Apparently."

"Then I make no promises." At her scowl, he held her chin and lowered his mouth to hers. "Laughing, smiling, loving," he said softly. "I want all of that with you. On our wedding day and every day afterward." He kissed her. "I fall more in love with you every second."

Lainey showed her approval with a long, slow kiss that had him backing her up against the copier. Her giggle broke their kiss. "Tucker, we can't. Lillian will be back any second."

"Then when can we?"

"As soon as I get back from picking out my wedding dress." She smiled up at him. "Wanna crash my bridal shower with me?"

"Do I have to go shopping too?"

She shook her head.

"Then what are we waiting for?"

Three weeks later Tucker stood in the white, flower-decked gazebo located in the center of the park. He swore the whole town had turned out for the wedding. He peered through the milling, chattering throng and waited for his bride to make her appearance. All voices hushed as the organist began the wedding march.

He held his breath as the crowd parted.

Sunshine poured down through a sudden parting in the clouds, bathing Lillian in a golden light as she stepped to the end of the red carpeting that had been rolled across the grass to the gazebo steps. Her dress was nothing short of stunning. *Short* being the operative word. And pink. Shocking was the shade that came to Tucker's mind.

Then Lillian moved down the carpet and took her place as maid of honor. On the arm of her aunt, who wore a more matronly version of Lillian's outfit, Lainey was a beautiful vision in a smartly tailored cream-colored silk suit worn with a lacy rose-colored shell.

As she walked toward him, Tucker thought about the more traditional life he'd wanted. He looked out over the congregation, then back at his soon-to-be wife, who winked at him as if to say she knew exactly what he was thinking. She probably did. There was nothing remotely traditional about the woman and the life he'd chosen. And that suited him perfectly.

THE EDITORS' CORNER

Ladies, step back! This July, LOVESWEPT is hotter than ever, with a month full of beguiling heroes and steamy romance. We managed to capture four Rebels with a Cause for your reading pleasure. There's Jack, a rough-and-tough detective with a glint in his eye; Luke, an architect who has to prove his innocence to win the heart of his woman; Clint, an FBI renegade with a score to settle; and Mitch, an ex–Navy Seal who's determined to earn back the life he left behind.

Beautiful Alex Sheridan and sexy Luke Morgan pack a lifetime of passion into **JUST ONE NIGHT**, LOVESWEPT #898, Eve Gaddy's sexy tale of two strangers who are trying to forget the past. As an officer on the Dallas bomb squad, Alex is called in to investigate the bombing of a construction site. All leads point to Luke, the architect on the project: he's a trained explosives expert; a large amount of money mysteriously shows up in his account; *and* he's the son of a convicted terrorist. As the hunt for the bomber continues, Alex and Luke are in too deep to keep their relationship on a professional basis. Alex had feared she'd never be able to trust herself again, but will Luke convince her that her instincts about him are right? Eve Gaddy pulls at the heartstrings in this moving story of a man who's backed against a wall and the woman who's willing to risk everything to save him.

In **A SCENT OF EDEN**, LOVESWEPT #899, Cynthia Powell demonstrates the delicious power of unlikely attractions. When Eden Wellbourne's fiancé goes missing, it's up to her to find the culprit. To that end, she hires Jack Rafferty, a man who is reputed to have an unmatched expertise in locating missing persons, a man who is clearly living on the edge. Meanwhile, Jack is having the second-worst day of his life, and he's definitely not in the mood to deal with the uptown girl standing on his doorstep. With his cash flow at an all-time low, however, he reluctantly decides to take on her case. Both are confused at the physical pull they feel toward each other, but neither wants to act on it first. When a break-in convinces Eden her own life is in danger, she turns to Jack for more than just his people-finding talents. Everything comes up roses when Cynthia Powell crosses a down-on-his-luck tough guy with a perfume princess.

Next, Jill Shalvis offers **LOVER COME BACK**, LOVESWEPT #900. As the editor of the *Heather Bay Daily News*, Justine Miller makes it her business to know what's happening in her town. But nothing could have prepared her for the shock of seeing her long-lost husband again. Not to mention the fact that he's the proud new owner of her newspaper. Two years earlier, Justine had anxiously waited for her new husband to return to their honeymoon suite. Only, Mitch Conner had disappeared, leaving Justine to deal with the embarrassment and pain. Mitch had had no choice but to leave her, but now he's back and more than eager to reclaim the love of his life. Justine refuses to believe his cockamamy story of corruption and witness protection programs. She has had her taste of marriage and love, and she's through with it. Mitch faces the toughest assignment of his life—proving to her that he'll never leave her. Jill Shalvis delivers a story of true love that can stand the test of time.

Finally, Karen Leabo brings us **THE DEVIL AND THE DEEP BLUE SEA**, LOVESWEPT #901. FBI agent Clint Nichols has a plan. Not a well-thought-out plan, but a plan nonetheless. He's going to kidnap a sister to exchange for an ex-wife. But the minute he boards the *Fortune's Smile*, Clint knows this mission will be a bust. His pretty quarry, Marissa Gabriole, pulls a gun on him and his getaway boat sinks. He's also hampered by a hurricane on the way and an accomplice who's a moron. Marissa soon grows tired of being on the run and chooses to team up with her kidnapper to flush out a mob boss. Clint isn't sure whether he can trust Marissa, but he knows it's the only way to wrap up an extensive undercover operation. Besides, what more does he have to lose? His life, for one thing. His heart, for another. Karen Leabo expertly blurs the line between what's right and what's love in this fast-paced, seaworthy caper.

Happy reading!

Susann Brailey *Joy Abella*

Susann Brailey   Joy Abella

Senior Editor   Administrative Editor

P.S. Look for these women's fiction titles coming in August! Sara Donati makes her fiction debut with the hardcover publication of **INTO THE WILDERNESS,** a magnificent reading experience set in the world of *Last of the Mohicans.* Now in paperback is Glenna McReynold's **THE CHALICE AND THE BLADE,** "an enthralling, exhilarating rush of a read" (Amanda Quick) in which a runaway bride and a feared sorcerer join in a spellbinding adventure of magic and passion. In **THE LONG SHOT,** the talented and humorous Michelle Martin presents a delightful cast of characters in a story about two sisters—and one man. Susan Krinard returns with **BODY AND SOUL,** an enchanting new romance about a love so deep it will bring a man and a woman together—in another century, another life. And Leslie LaFoy follows up with **LADY RECKLESS,** as lovers fleeing across Ireland are locked in a fight for their lives and their love . . . and a fight against the Fates themselves. And immediately following this page, preview the Bantam women's fiction titles on sale in July.

For current information on Bantam's women's fiction, visit our website at the following address:
http://www.bdd.com/romance

Don't miss these extraordinary
novels from Bantam Books!

On sale in July:

WHEN VENUS FELL
by Deborah Smith

FINDING LAURA
by Kay Hooper

When Venus Fell
BY DEBORAH SMITH

*Read on for a preview of Deborah Smith's new
heartwarming novel . . .*

The stranger caught my attention like a trumpet player
blowing a high C in the middle of a harp solo.

I always drew up in a knot when a certain type of
man watched Ella and me in public. Over the years I'd
developed a knack for pinpointing the kind who considered himself the guardian of truth, justice, and the
American way. But this one stood out more than usual,
particularly in the Hers Truly. After all, he was the only
masculine patron I'd ever seen in the audience. In fact
he looked like the kind of man who'd been born with
more than an ordinary share of testosterone.

I blinked then stared again through the haze of
stage lights and cigarette smoke. *Holy freakin' moly*, as
we used to say at St. Cecilia's, when the nuns weren't
listening.

He was tall, dark and yes, bluntly handsome. But
badly worn around the edges. His face was gaunt, his
skin was pale enough to show a beard shadow even in
dim light, his mouth was appealing but too tight. He
was watching me as if I were doing a strip tease and he
was an off-duty vice cop.

Frowning, he pulled a dog-eared black-and-white
photo from his shirt pocket and held it out. For the
first time I noticed his right hand. I froze. Whoever he
was, something godawful had happened to him.

His ring finger and little finger were gone, as well
as a deep section of the knuckles at their base. His

middle finger was scarred and knotty. Lines of pink scar tissue and deep, puckered gouges snaked up his right forearm. Grotesque and awkward, the hand looked like a deformed claw.

Suddenly I was aware of my own fingers, flexing them, grateful they were all in place. He wasn't an invincible threat. He was very human, and more than a little damaged.

"Enjoying the view?" he asked tersely. I jerked my gaze to his face. Ruddy blotches of anger and embarrassment colored his cheeks. He quickly transferred the photo to his undamaged left hand and dropped the right hand into the shadows between his knees. "Have you ever seen a copy of this picture before?"

I took a deep breath and looked at the photo. A solemn, handsome young boy gazed back at me from my parents' wedding picture. There was only one copy of the picture, I thought, and I still had it. "Where did you get that?"

"It's been in my family."

"Who? What family?"

"The Camerons."

I leaned toward him, scrutinizing him helplessly. "Who *are* you?"

He pointed to the boy. "Gib Cameron," he said. "Does that mean anything to you?"

My head reeled. When I was a child I'd decided I'd never meet Gib Cameron in person but I would love him forever. That childhood memory had become a shrine to all the lost innocence in my life.

But now the shrine was real. *He* was real. "I remember your name," I said with a shrug.

"I remember yours," he said flatly. "And it's not Ann Nelson."

Gib Cameron had finally found me. It was appropriate that he knew who I really was. After all, he'd named me before I was born.

"Why are you here?" I asked warily.

He smiled with no humor. "I'm going to make you an offer you can't refuse."

MIRROR, MIRROR ON THE WALL
WHO'S THE DEADLIEST ONE OF ALL?

Finding Laura
by bestselling author
KAY HOOPER

It's an antique mirror that can reveal secrets . . . or tarnish the truth. And for struggling artist Laura Sutherland buying it is only the first step into a dark maze of lies, manipulation—and murder. It brings Peter Kilbourne into her life and makes her the prime suspect in his fatal stabbing. Determined to clear her name—and uncover Peter's reason for wanting the mirror back—Laura will breach the iron gates of the Kilbourne estate. There she will find that each family member has something to hide. Which one of them looks in the mirror and sees the reflection of the killer? And which one will choose Laura to be the next to die?

"Kay Hooper is a multitalented author whose stories always pack a tremendous punch."
—Iris Johansen,
New York Times bestselling author

It was after five o'clock that evening when the security guard downstairs called up to tell Laura that she had a visitor.

"Who is it, Larry?"

"It's Mr. Peter Kilbourne, Miss Sutherland," the guard replied, unaware of the shock he was delivering. "He says it's in reference to the mirror you bought today."

For just an instant, Laura was conscious of nothing except an overwhelming urge to grab her mirror and run. It was nothing she could explain, but the panic was so real that Laura went ice-cold with it. Thankfully, the reaction was short-lived, since her rational mind demanded to know why on earth she felt so threatened. After all, she had bought the mirror legally, and no one had the right to take it away from her. Not even Peter Kilbourne.

Trying to shake off uneasiness, she said, "Thank you, Larry. Send him up, please."

She found her shoes and stepped into them, and absently smoothed a few strands of hair that had escaped from the long braid hanging down her back, but Laura didn't think or worry too much about how she looked. Instead, as she waited for her unexpected visitor, she stood near the couch and kept glancing at the mirror lying on several layers of newspaper on the coffee table.

It looked now, after hours of hard work, like an entirely different mirror. The rich, warm, reddish gold color of old brass gleamed now, and the elaborate pattern stamped into the metal, a shade darker, showed up vividly. It was a curious pattern, not floral as with most of the mirrors she had found, but rather a swirling series of loops and curves that were, Laura had discovered, actually made up of one continuous line—rather like a maze.

It was around the center of this maze that Laura had discovered the numbers or letters stamped into the brass, but since she hadn't yet finished polishing the back, she still didn't know what, if anything, the writing signified.

A quiet knock at her door recalled her thoughts, and Laura mentally braced herself as she went to greet her visitor. She had no particular image in her mind of

Peter Kilbourne, but she certainly didn't expect to open her door to the most handsome man she'd ever seen.

It was an actual, physical shock to see him, she realized dimly, a stab of the same astonishment one would feel if a statue of masculine perfection suddenly breathed and smiled. He was the epitome of tall, dark, and handsome—and more. Much more. Black hair, pale blue eyes, a flashing smile. Perfect features. And his charm was an almost visible thing, somehow, obvious even before he spoke in a deep, warm voice.

"Miss Sutherland? I'm Peter Kilbourne."

A voice to break hearts.

Laura gathered her wits and stepped back, opening the door wider to admit him. "Come in." She thought he was about her own age, maybe a year or two older.

He came into the apartment and into the living room, taking in his surroundings quickly but thoroughly, and clearly taking note of the mirror on the coffee table. His gaze might have widened a bit when it fell on her collection of mirrors, but Laura couldn't be sure, and when he turned to face her, he was smiling with every ounce of his charm.

It was unsettling how instantly and powerfully she was affected by that magnetism. Laura had never considered herself vulnerable to charming men, but she knew without doubt that this one would be difficult to resist—whatever it was he wanted of her. Too uneasy to sit down or invite him to, Laura merely stood with one hand on the back of a chair and eyed him with what she hoped was a faint, polite smile.

If Peter Kilbourne thought she was being ungracious in not inviting him to sit down, he didn't show it. He gestured slightly toward the coffee table and said, "I see you've been hard at work, Miss Sutherland."

She managed a shrug. "It was badly tarnished. I wanted to get a better look at the pattern."

He nodded, his gaze tracking past her briefly to once again note the collection of mirrors near the hallway. "You have quite a collection. Have you . . . always collected mirrors?"

It struck her as an odd question somehow, perhaps because there was something hesitant in his tone, something a bit surprised in his eyes. But Laura replied truthfully despite another stab of uneasiness. "Since I was a child, actually. So you can see why I bought that one today at the auction."

"Yes." He slid his hands into the pockets of his dark slacks, sweeping open his suit jacket as he did so in a pose that might have been studied or merely relaxed. "Miss Sutherland—look, do you mind if I call you Laura?"

"No, of course not."

"Thank you," he nodded gravely, a faint glint of amusement in his eyes recognizing her reluctance. "I'm Peter."

She nodded in turn, but didn't speak.

"Laura, would you be interested in selling the mirror back to me? At a profit, naturally."

"I'm sorry." She was shaking her head even before he finished speaking. "I don't want to sell the mirror."

"I'll give you a hundred for it."

Laura blinked in surprise, but again shook her head. "I'm not interested in making money, Mr. Kilbourne—"

"Peter."

A little impatiently, she said, "All right—Peter. I don't want to sell the mirror. And I did buy it legitimately."

"No one's saying you didn't, Laura," he soothed. "And you aren't to blame for my mistake, certainly.

Look, the truth is that the mirror shouldn't have been put up for auction. It's been in my family a long time, and we'd like to have it back. Five hundred."

Not a bad profit on a five-dollar purchase. She drew a breath and spoke slowly. "No. I'm sorry, I really am, but . . . I've been looking for this—for a mirror like this—for a long time. To add to my collection. I'm not interested in making money, so please don't bother to raise your offer. Even five thousand wouldn't make a difference."

His eyes were narrowed slightly, very intent on her face, and when he smiled suddenly it was with rueful certainty. "Yes, I can see that. You don't have to look so uneasy, Laura—I'm not going to wrest the thing away from you by force."

"I never thought you would," she murmured, lying.

He chuckled, a rich sound that stroked along her nerve endings like a caress. "No? I'm afraid I've made you nervous, and that was never my intention. Why don't I buy you dinner some night as an apology?"

This man is dangerous. "That isn't necessary," she said.

"I insist."

Laura looked at his incredibly handsome face, that charming smile, and drew yet another deep breath. "Will your wife be coming along?" she asked mildly.

"If she's in town, certainly." His eyes were guileless.

Very dangerous. Laura shook her head. "Thanks, but no apology is necessary. You offered a generous price for the mirror; I refused. That's all there is to it." She half turned and made a little gesture toward the door with one hand, unmistakably inviting him to leave.

Peter's beautiful mouth twisted a bit, but he obeyed the gesture and followed her to the door. When she opened it and stood back, he paused to reach into the inner pocket of his jacket and produced a business card. "Call me if you change your mind," he said. "About the mirror, I mean."

Or anything else, his smile said.

"I'll do that," she returned politely, accepting the card.

"It was nice meeting you, Laura."

"Thank you. Nice meeting you," she murmured.

He gave her a last flashing smile, lifted a hand slightly in a small salute, and left her apartment.

Laura closed the door and leaned back against it for a moment, relieved and yet still uneasy. She didn't know why Peter Kilbourne wanted the mirror back badly enough to pay hundreds of dollars for it, but every instinct told her the matter was far from settled.

She hadn't heard the last of him.

On sale in August:

INTO THE WILDERNESS
by Sara Donati

THE CHALICE AND THE BLADE
by Glenna McReynolds

BODY AND SOUL
by Susan Krinard

THE LONG SHOT
by Michelle Martin

LADY RECKLESS
by Leslie Lafoy

Jean Stone

FIRST LOVES

For every woman there is a first love, the love she never forgets. Now Meg, Zoe, and Alissa have given themselves six months to find the men who got away. But can they recover the magic they left behind?

_____56343-2 $5.99/$6.99

PLACES BY THE SEA

In the bestselling tradition of Barbara Delinsky, this is the enthralling , emotionally charged tale of a woman who thought she led a charmed life...until she discovered the real meaning of friendship, betrayal, forgiveness, and love.

_____57424-8 $5.99/$7.99